Mystery Repeats Itself
A MINERVA BIGGS MYSTERY

CORDELIA ROOK

Copyright © 2022 by Cordelia Rook

Cover Design © 2021 by Wicked Good Book Covers

All rights reserved.

ISBN: 9798424657863

No part of this book may be reproduced in any form or by any electronic or mechanical means, including information storage and retrieval systems, without written permission from the author, except for the use of brief quotations in a book review.

❦ Created with Vellum

Chapter One

WHATEVER PODSNAPPERY they would have you believe, the truth is that new beginnings are a big old pain. Case in point: that time my new boss hit me in the face and kicked my dog.

It was my first day. *The* first day. I could not have been more steeped in hope if you'd stuck me in a teabag and tossed me in an ocean of it. I'd come half a state away from almost everybody who knew me—or knew about me. It was my fresh start, my blank slate, my whatever other cliché you care to apply to what amounted to, really, running away from home.

But you know what they say about the things you try to outrun. I guess that must be a different *they* from the *they* who encourage new beginnings.

I would have been grateful for the chance to run anywhere. Baird House was just butter upon bacon, with its famous rhododendrons, its signature red roof. The elaborate stonework, pale gray gargoyles and ravens looking down at me from shadowed nooks and corners.

This wasn't just my fresh start (etc.), it was a *genuine Gilded Age mansion*. And as personal assistant to the Baird family, I was going to be *living in it*.

I still remember that giddy feeling I got, the first time I crossed the threshold. It was Snick who gave me and Plant our introductory tour. And no, that is not a typo, and no, I do not mean Nick. Snick was the only name I ever knew for the Bairds' household manager (never *butler*, Mrs. B did not tolerate the use of servant words). I never found out how he came by it; for all his love of gossip and pantry politicking, he was pretty close about his own life. But in my head it was short for Snicker, which would have been apt. That one had some sass in him.

Introductory tour highlight/lowlight: The highlight was the most magnificent library I'd ever seen. Velvety fabrics, plush rugs, and pretty much anywhere your eye landed, it landed on a book. Or twelve. Walking into that room was like walking into a warm kitchen and a cool porch, both at once. It was like coming home, but not the regular kind of home. The safe kind, that maybe only exists in fiction. I immediately decided its very existence was a good omen.

Even Plant loved it, and tried to register his approval by hopping up onto a creamy-chocolate-colored loveseat for a nap. Upon discovering that not only was he unwelcome on the furniture, but he was to have no nap at all, and was furthermore expected to *climb stairs*, he gave me his very judgiest look and shoved his ears back so far anybody looking at him head-on would've thought he was earless. Maybe I should've taken that as a bad omen for the lowlight to come.

That would be the second floor, which was where The Incident happened.

A long gallery served as the main hallway upstairs. Snick walked me down it slowly, the better to admire the photographs. I nodded at one, a crowd of people dressed in formal clothes—early twentieth century, at a glance—and old-timey masquerade masks. "The first ball?" I asked.

Snick confirmed that it was. "September 1913," he said. "It's usually family portraits up here, but they always bring out the ball pictures this time of year. There's a huge version of that one that goes in the ballroom on the day."

I cocked my head, studying the picture. "But this would have to be Tybryd's ballroom, not the one here." Tybryd (*Rhymes with hybrid!* as its staff was so fond of chirping at new arrivals) was Alistair Baird's real triumph of robber-baron excess. At two hundred and fifty rooms, it had once been the biggest private dwelling in the country, before starting its second life as a luxury resort. By contrast, the little cottage we stood in, built for Alistair's mother on the outskirts of his grand estate, boasted only seventy rooms.

"Yeah, the ball was held at Tybryd for something like forty years," said Snick. "It was Clifford's father who moved it here, after he converted the big house to a hotel. They like to keep the boundary between business and personal firm." He rolled his eyes. "Or they think it makes the party seem more exclusive and important if it's at their personal home, take your pick."

My pick was the second one, but I decided to keep that to myself. I pointed at another picture. "Is that from the first ball, too?"

He nodded. "Alistair and Emily Baird, minus their masks."

I'd never seen such a clear photo of Emily Baird before, and I was instantly enthralled. Her face was a contradiction, both expressive and closed; as if she knew a lot of secrets, but wasn't about to tell them to the likes of you. She looked like an elegantly coiffed mom, like she'd smack you with a wooden spoon if you got out of line. But the ghost of a smile haunted her lips.

Alistair was pretty boring by comparison. He mostly just looked old and cranky, but I guessed that was fair, since he'd have been a bit of both that night. By all accounts cranky was his default state, and he was in his fifties (an age that seemed distant to my twenty-eight-year-old self) in 1913. Even Tybryd was sixteen years old by then. "He always has the meanest look on his face," I said.

"Always?" Snick raised a brow so pale it was almost invisible. I was pretty sure he plucked it. You did not come by an arch like that naturally. "You guys hang out a lot, or?"

I shrugged. "I'm a history person. I've studied."

"Mrs. B will love that." He gestured for me to keep following him, and I smacked my thigh for Plant to fall in line. Which Plant was happy to do, as he was finding this most recent stop supremely boring.

"They have a home gym down this hall," Snick said as we rounded a corner, "but don't get any ideas about using it. They really don't like people up here on their private floor. That's this door here. And down at the end—"

He never got to tell me what was down at the end, because at that moment the door he'd just pointed out swung open.

Abruptly, and right into my face.

I squealed and put my hands up to my nose, all the while struggling not to lose my less-than-legendary balance. That door was heavy.

Plant lunged forward, prepared to defend me against whatever vicious attacker was upon us.

"... original is completely gone, right? It can't be traced or restored or anything like that?" An older but still handsome man emerged from the other side of the door, talking on his phone. He was so preoccupied, and it had happened so quickly, he didn't even seem to notice he'd hit me. Until, that is, Plant made his displeasure clear.

Plant had some training as a guard dog; he knew how to warn people. I'll admit that he had what you could call a confident snarl. And I will further allow that a confidently snarling giant black dog might be construed, by some, as threatening.

Even so. Snarl was all he did.

And that's when Clifford Baird, hotel magnate, extremely rich person, and my brand new boss, for all the heavens to witness, *kicked my dog*.

So much for my fresh start. I was clearly going to have to kill the man.

∼

CLIFFORD STEADFASTLY MAINTAINED that he had not, in fact, kicked my dog.

"It was a push," he insisted, not for the first time since we'd closed ourselves away in his first-floor office. We'd not gotten around to sitting down, except for Plant, who was lounging quite comfortably under Clifford's antique boat of a desk. "A nudge, really. With my knee, not my foot. It's not even possible to kick a thing without your foot."

Had he just referred to Plant as *a thing*? This was not making me view the situation more kindly. I gave him my signature teacher's Countenance of Disapproval.

Which he either didn't see, or disregarded entirely. "I think we can agree to define that as a nudge," he went on. "And I had to get him off me, didn't I?"

"He wasn't on you," I pointed out. "He was near you, which is a completely different thing. He wasn't going to escalate, as long as you didn't. He was just trying to protect me, and you can't really blame him for that." I raised the ice pack off my face long enough to gesture at my nose.

"An accident," Clifford said, also not for the first time. He nodded at Plant. "Anyway, he doesn't look traumatized, does he?"

Plant confirmed his lack of trauma with two thumps of his tail. And really, who was I kidding, he probably hadn't even particularly noticed Clifford's so-called nudge. You could've dropped an anvil on that boy's big dumb head, and only had a fifty-fifty shot at him noticing.

Still. Big dumb head notwithstanding, we were not off to the sort of start I'd been dreaming of.

I sighed. I'd been nervous all along about bringing a dog like Plant into a house like this. A little one, like you could keep in your purse, sure. But a dog with a three-digit weight and not-insignificant jowls seemed a tad out of place. Those seventy rooms I mentioned? Not one of them looked like the kind you'd want a dog drooling all over. And it wasn't like personal assistants were so hard to come by, or required such a rare skill set, that the Bairds couldn't have found somebody dogless to fill the role.

But everybody I'd interviewed with—Clifford, Mrs. B, Snick, then Clifford twice more—had been so insistent that Plant would be welcome. More than welcome, in fact. I was assured that having a dog was considered a plus for this position. Apparently Mrs. B had lost the last of her beloved shelties a few months before, and Clifford was hoping Plant's presence would scratch the itch left behind, lest she go out and get herself a half dozen more.

And now look at us. Not two hours in, and they'd already beat us both up.

"Okay. Minerva." Clifford said both words as if they were standalone statements of some kind, and drew out the *er* in *Minerva* in a way that he maybe meant to be conciliatory, but that was actually patronizing as all blazes. "We've obviously gotten off on the wrong foot here. But your first day isn't officially until tomorrow. It would be pretty poor form for me to fire you before you even start, after you drove all this way. Don't you think?"

I blinked at him. "Fire me?"

When had *that* been put on the table? As my self-pitying inner monologue could have told him, *we* were the injured parties here.

"Well, your dog did attack me," Clifford said, then went right on talking over my strangled sound of outrage. "And he is a very big dog." He held up his hands. "But let's not let this get any more unpleasant than it already has, or needs to be, what do you say? Why don't we give it another try?"

He took a step closer to me, which brought him about a step and a half too close. I crossed my arms, but did not step back. I was not to know Clifford Baird for long, but I learned pretty quickly—right in that room, in fact—how much he enjoyed slapping a veneer of good humor over subtle intimidation. He liked his opponents off balance, and as far as he was concerned, everybody was an opponent.

"Wonderful!" Clifford gave me a big, fake smile with his big, fake teeth. "Bessie would like you to join the family for dinner tonight, so you can get to know everyone. The kids haven't met you yet, have they?"

"No. Snick didn't think any of you all were home." *Seeing as it's Monday afternoon, and you supposedly have jobs*, I added, but only in my head. I hadn't thought anybody was home, either. And it had certainly come as a surprise to my nose.

There wasn't much way we could have anticipated

Clifford coming out that door; the gym was soundproofed. Evidently Mrs. B did not enjoy the sound of her son Percy slamming weights down at six in the morning. Why they would have a room like that on the second floor at all, when such a thing clearly belonged in a basement or a garage, was beyond me. You would think a person interested in exercise wouldn't mind walking down a few flights of stairs.

"Yes, well," said Clifford, "Tybryd's gym manager is putting in an order for some new equipment soon, and I wanted to check whether one of the rowing machines he's replacing would fit in our gym here. So dinner is all settled, then. You'll meet everyone. Tristan's in town, too, for the ball."

"I heard." Heard, and memorized: The Bairds had four adult children. Percy and Elaine lived at home, despite being thirty and thirty-one, respectively. I guessed the trajectory into adulthood was kind of different when home was a mansion. Both worked for the family business. Gwen was estranged from her parents and, Snick warned me, Never To Be Spoken Of. Something about her marrying somebody Clifford considered unsuitable, and a subsequent all-family explosion. And Tristan, who was only vaguely and occasionally employed, always came home for the entire month of September, for a nice mountain vacation and the annual costume ball.

More than a century down the line and they still called it a ball, like they were living in a fairytale or a Regency romance. It was a very big deal—to them, anyway. As far as I could tell, it was a lot of sound and fury that didn't signify much of anything, but at least they picked a charity to fundraise for every year.

It was also the main reason they'd been so eager for me to start right away. The ball was almost three weeks away, but preparations had already risen to frenzy level, and losing their last PA at such a time had been a dire blow. Mostly, I suspected, to Snick.

"Bring Plant to the dining room," Clifford went on. "Bessie would be very disappointed if you didn't. Seven o'clock. You know where the dining room is?"

"I can find it." I actually wasn't as confident of that as you might think. Baird House, having been lived in continuously for a hundred and twenty-odd years, had seen quite a few remodels and improvements, none of which appeared to have been done with any sort of regard for the prior ones. The result was a disjointed maze.

Part of its charm, as far as I was concerned. In contrast to Mr. Clifford Baird, who had no discernible charms at all. Despite his clear opinion to the contrary.

But I'd only lived there for an hour, and as I might have mentioned, I was a bit on the desperate side with respect to starting a new life. Plus there weren't exactly a lot of openings for a live-in position right in the middle of history. Where they would let you bring your gigantic dog, no less. The chance to live in a place like this, to work for the Baird estate and Tybryd, was a dream.

So maybe Clifford was just that one necessary thing that kept it from being too good to be true. If he hadn't been a hornswaggling ratbag with a false smile and cold eyes, I might have had to be suspicious of how perfect the whole thing was.

Really, him kicking my dog was kind of a good thing, if you thought about it the right way.

"Thank you," I said. "I'll be there."

I just had to hope the rest of the Bairds were better than this one.

Chapter Two

PLANT and I left my little bedroom on the third floor (*staff level*, never *servants' quarters*) fifteen minutes ahead of dinner, just in case I really did get lost on the way to the dining room. Except I didn't (much), so we got there twelve minutes early. It looked like a campy-drama-about-rich-people movie set: super long table, about a million chairs, crackling fire. Flowers everywhere. Pastels. So many pastels.

And a man, broad-shouldered and dark-haired, leaning against the wall near the fireplace. His head was bent over his phone, but he looked up when Plant bounded into the room. His face was kind, like his mother's.

But those dimples could've been copied and pasted from his father. Not that this guy's big smile was for me —he didn't seem to notice me at all.

"You must be Plantagenet!" He squatted down and threw his arms wide. Needing no further encouragement, Plant launched himself at the man. The man, in turn, gave Plant scritches with dangerous enthusiasm.

I say dangerous because nothing delighted Plant quite so much as having a fuss made over him. And a delighted Plant could be ... let's call it ungainly. He immediately broke into his signature wiggle, a full-body wag the likes of which the uninitiated would only believe if they saw it for themselves. When the man who had to be either Tristan or Percy Baird laughed and clapped at him, I knew what would come next.

I mean, not specifically, but I had a good general idea. I called out a warning about getting him too excited. Neither of them paid me the least bit of mind.

Plant turned around and, finding himself close to the end of the table, snatched up a napkin in his big slobbery jaws, sending a couple of forks flying in the process. He then pranced back and forth in front of his new friend, certain his prize would make him all the more admired.

He'd been doing it since he was a puppy. Whenever I came home, or had a guest, or Plant met somebody new he particularly liked, he would find something—a toy or bone, his collar, an oven mitt, whatever was handy—to show off. Lengthy exclamations as to the very niceness of the item were expected.

"Plant! That's very nice, now leave it!" I stopped juggling the forks long enough to lunge for his collar. He sidestepped me handily. He'd been doing that since he was a puppy, too.

This was the part where, if I gave the slightest indication of chasing him, he would run. And a lumbering beast like him, in a room like that, could not mean anything good for the china or the bottles of wine. I went still and repeated, calmly, my request that he leave it.

But Tristan-or-Percy was more agile than I was, and Plant had less practice at eluding him. While Plant had his eye on me, the unnamed Baird deftly grabbed his collar with one hand and retrieved the napkin with the other. He wadded up the latter, which was looking considerably wetter for the wear, and put it on the sideboard rather than back on the table.

"Sit," I hissed at Plant, then, in a much kinder tone, said, "I am so sorry. He's still pretty young yet, and he, um, loves meeting new people."

That wasn't entirely true. He did love meeting some people, but he could be selective. Apparently this guy had passed Plant's rigorous testing process, which I suspected mostly involved how partial to dogs the person was.

"Don't worry about it, he's fine. Aren't you, buddy? I'm Percy, by the way." With a final scratch behind Plant's ears, Percy-by-the-way straightened up, wiped his hands on his pants, then looked fully at me for the first time since I'd come into the room.

And said, in a tone I can only describe as disgusted, "Oh, for crying out loud."

Needless to say, I was a tad befuddled. And maybe more than a tad annoyed. Plant galumphing around this formally appointed room like a clown qualified as *fine*, but I had somehow earned a *for crying out loud*?

I crossed my arms. "Excuse me?"

He tossed a hand in my direction. I was shortly to learn that he did that a lot. Percy Baird was a great gesticulator. "Where did he find you?"

"I assume you mean Clifford?" I used my chilliest tone, of which I don't mind saying I was pretty proud. It scared most people, and this nitwit deserved it. "I'm Minerva, by the way. Lovely to meet you."

He didn't look scared, but he at least had the grace to look embarrassed as he extended his hand. I shook it with a firm grip, to cure him of any notion that I was somebody to be trifled with.

"Yeah, I saw your name floating around in some emails," he said. "But I thought there might have been a typo. Is it Minerva Briggs?"

I knew just where this was going. I shook my head. "Biggs."

"Really?"

"Yep."

"Not a typo, then."

"Not if it was spelled B-I-G-G-S."

"So your name is Minnie Biggs." Just to make sure I didn't miss the pun, I guessed, he bounced his index finger back and forth to emphasize the words. "Mini ... Bigs."

I threw my eyes wide in feigned surprise and admiration. "Odsbodikins! Nobody's ever pointed that out before!"

To his credit, he laughed instead of taking offense. It was a likable, pleasant laugh. The kind you wanted to hear again, which was somewhat at odds with my newly formed determination to dislike him. "Did you just say *odsbodikins*?" he asked.

"Oh. Yeah." I cleared my throat, feeling a little like a

weirdo. Which was annoying, because if anybody was the weirdo, this guy was the weirdo. "Victorian slang was kind of a thing between me and my sister when we were kids, and I've never broken the habit."

Thoroughly disappointed that we'd become so boring, Plant heaved a sigh and flopped down against the sideboard. The momentary interruption was enough to break me out of my distraction, and bring my thoughts back to the subject at hand. Namely, Percy Baird's rudeness.

"And to answer your question," I said, straightening my shoulders, "your father found me in more or less the usual way. It's true that I had an inside contact, Tybryd's HR director is married to my high school boyfriend, but I—"

"You dated Paul Kwon?"

I blinked. "You know him?"

"Small town, the clichés are true," Percy said with a shrug. "Everybody knows everybody."

I frowned at that. Sure, Bryd Hollow was a small town. But it had originally been established to support the estate; in other words, it had originally been populated by servants. And I wasn't sure things had changed all that much. I didn't see the Bairds as townies. "Even you?"

"Yep." He stuffed his hands into his pockets. "My mother has a lot of rules to teach us that our money doesn't make us any better than anybody else."

I glanced around that ridiculously expensive dining room and tried (not very hard) to keep a straight face. "Does she?"

Percy followed my gaze, and did not try (at all) to keep a straight face. There were those dimples again. "She picks her battles, I guess. But no fancy boarding schools or private schools for us. I went to the local public schools with everybody else. So, you and Paul …?"

"Are still friendly. I asked Carrie a few months ago to keep an eye out for any openings I might be a good fit for, and—"

"Are you a good fit, though? I heard you're a teacher."

Apparently all those lessons in humility hadn't taught Percy not to interrupt people. I pursed my lips at him, no doubt looking a lot like the teacher he'd just accused me of being. "I'll have you know I'm extremely well-organized. And proficient with all the tech you use. I interviewed with your father and your mother and Snick, and they were all perfectly satisfied with my qualifications."

Percy snorted. "I'll bet he was."

"I beg your pardon?" I was trying very hard to cling to all that optimism I'd woken up with, but the last of it was fading fast. According to Snick, Percy was the best and brightest of the Baird family, a claim that was now concerning me greatly.

"I'm sorry," he said. "This is a bad start, isn't it? I'm being awful."

"Well, you're not being great."

"It's just, I really should have insisted on interviewing you myself." Percy rubbed the back of his neck with one hand and waved at me with the other, all the while looking supremely annoyed. "You're very pretty."

"I'm ... did ... *what*?" I was honestly speechless. Not only did I not know what to say, I didn't even know what I wanted to say. I wasn't even saying anything in my head.

Maybe because I was devoting so much energy to resisting touching my hair. Like many women, I had my share of insecurities. I was too short and scrawny. If only my gray eyes had leaned blue or green, instead of stubbornly sticking to the color of a miserable sky on a miserable day. If my brown-bordering-on-chestnut hair had been a little redder, or a little bit curly. I did not think of myself as *very pretty*.

Percy Baird though, now he was pretty. Dorky, certainly. Lacking any and all control over what came out of his mouth, apparently. But he had very nice hands, and that smile was downright arresting. I might have been flattered by the compliment, from a man like that.

You know, if it hadn't been so wildly inappropriate. And delivered like a citation.

He still hadn't followed it up with anything. Was he expecting me to mount some sort of defense? I gestured at him. "Are you waiting for me to say something? Because I'm kind of waiting for you to explain yourself."

"I'm sorry." He gave me a sheepish look that I steadfastly did not find endearing. "Permission to speak freely?"

I raised my brows. "This wasn't you speaking freely up to this point?"

"I'm sorry."

"You seem to be sorry a lot."

Percy looked down at Plant, who thumped his tail in return, the traitor. "This is an awkward conversation to have. But I guess it's better to have it than not. I asked my father to hire a man this time."

"I beg your—"

"Or at least somebody ugly."

"—*pardon?*"

"Just to be on the safe side. He has an eye for pretty girls." He winced. "Women! I meant women, not girls. Sor—"

"Sorry, yes, I know you are. And he hasn't behaved at all inappropriately with me." I tilted my head and amended that. "Well, he did almost break my nose."

"He *what*?"

"Never mind. Are you saying I need to be worried?"

"No, no, it's not like that." Percy shook his head a couple of extra times, presumably as evidence that he was being extra honest. "It's not a harassment thing, it's always been ... well, there've been some affairs over the years. It's ... I come from a long line of philanderers."

He misinterpreted my burst of laughter and held up his hands, as if to demonstrate that he was not about to accost me on the spot. "Don't worry, it gets better with every generation."

I waved that away. As far as I was concerned, the present generation of Bairds took a backseat to century-old gossip. "Are you saying Alistair Baird, a man so pious he built Bryd Hollow around a church and named all its streets after virtues, was a womanizer?"

"And an adulterer." Percy sucked his breath in through his teeth, like a disappointed dad. "You won't find that in any of his bios, it's a pretty well-kept secret. So I hope I can count on your discretion. But if it helps your shattered illusion any, he did feel really bad about it every time. Lots of penance and whatnot."

Interesting. This man wasn't shy about openly calling his father a womanizer, and asked for no such discretion where that was concerned. But protecting the reputation of the founder of the dynasty was apparently a priority.

Percy shot a glance at the doorway before looking back at me and lowering his voice. "Anyway, listen, if you should happen to have any trouble with my father, you know, if he should ... bother you at all, I hope you'll come to me right away."

"What I would do right away is put a stop to it."

"Of course. I just meant—"

"What's all this whispering in here? Are you plotting something without us?" A woman with Percy's eyes but much lighter hair came strolling into the room, arm in arm with a man whose good-humored face was dominated by a pair of thick, shaggy brows. This could only be Elaine and Tristan.

No less than four fat French bulldogs followed at their heels, but they didn't stay there. As soon as they saw Plant, they launched themselves at him and immediately began climbing all over him, licking at his jowls. Plant accepted this unexpected display of affection with equanimity and a slow wag of his tail.

"I heard yours is friendly, yeah?" Tristan asked, then went on without waiting for an answer. "My babies are as sweet as they come. Even the ones whose names say the opposite. Sweetie, Saltie, Tart, and Bitts, meet your new friend. What is it? Palette? Bassinet? My mother told me, but she tells me so *many* things, you know? It's hard to keep even half of them straight."

"Plantagenet," I said. "Plant for short."

"Minnie Biggs and her animal named Plant," said Percy. Nobody else laughed, but that didn't stop him from enjoying a good chuckle all on his own. "Minerva, this is my brother Tristan, he doesn't live here, and my sister Elaine, she does. Guys, this is Minerva, the new PA."

"And thank goodness you're here!" Elaine offered me a gummy smile that struck me as almost as insincere as her father's. "I have so much I need help with, for the ball. I—"

"Can wait, I'm sure," Percy cut in. "She doesn't actually start until tomorrow. Mom invited her as a guest tonight, to get to know everybody."

Elaine rolled her eyes. "You're so bossy. Especially for a *kid* brother."

Tristan moved to my side and gave me a soft elbow. "They'll be bickering for the next while. He's got a lovely coat." He nodded down at Plant in all his glossy black glory. "What's he a mix of?"

"Your guess is as good," I said with a shrug. "Great Dane, lab, and mastiff, at least, but there could be something else in there."

Up close, Tristan's face was puffy in a way that suggested overindulgence, and he looked tired. But at least his smile was genuine. "I guess that explains his size. How much does he weigh?"

"About a hundred, give or take."

"Oh my gosh, he weighs how much?" Elaine stopped

arguing with Percy and craned her neck to look at Plant, as if really noticing him for the first time. "Have you had him DNA tested, to see what-all he is? You definitely should, if you haven't. Vets have no idea, you know, and neither do the shelters. Whoever you got him from probably just made stuff up."

Despite my deep indifference to Plant's pedigree, in the interest of manners I tried to look like I gave this suggestion actual consideration before answering. "Do you think? I'm not sure how accurate those tests are."

Elaine huffed. "How can DNA lie?"

"What DNA?" Clifford barked as he strode into the room. Which was weird—the barking, I mean, not the striding. I didn't know him well, of course, but I'd sized him up enough to think that barking wasn't his style. He seemed like more of a manipulator than a direct confronter. But the look he gave Elaine was actually ... angry? Maybe they'd had a fight earlier or something.

"Um ..." Elaine's confident expression instantly melted.

"What are you talking about?" Clifford pressed.

"Minerva's dog?"

Clifford scoffed and crabbed about wastes of time, and the kind of person who would care about a dog's DNA, and the way people would spend money on any foolish thing. While he was busy with that, Bessie Baird (who'd told me the second we were introduced, on a video call, that everyone called her Mrs. B, even some of her kids) walked in behind her husband.

"Mine*r*va!" She hurried over to me, alarming Plant a little, and took my hands in hers. "I'm *so* glad you're here!

And you look *adorable*!" She gave her sons a wide smile. "Isn't she just *adorable*?" Mrs. B always spoke in italics and exclamation points. You could practically see them in the air, like the speech bubbles they put over cartoon people's heads.

The motion to declare me adorable was unanimously passed, and Mrs. B moved on to making a fuss over the dogs. A maid (which was what they called the maids, I guessed they couldn't think of a non-servant word for that function) poured wine and brought out platter after platter of food. Finally everyone was seated, with Clifford at the head of the table and the dogs underneath it. Mrs. B made Percy move down a seat so that I could take the chair to her left, between them.

"This way we can get to know each other!" She gave my leg two enthusiastic little pats. I guessed I would be excited about everything too, if I had her life. Although maybe not so much if I had to be married to Clifford Baird to get it.

First dinner highlight/lowlight: The highlight was definitely the food. Rib roast that melted in the mouth, asparagus with shallots, stewed mushrooms, boiled potatoes drenched in butter, and freshly baked, slightly sweet rolls. If I could have done nothing but eat that meal in silence, I would have been the happiest of women.

But of course, that's not how family dinners work. It's hard to pinpoint the lowest light in that conversation, so I'll just call the lowlight the conversation in general.

At first it was mainly Mrs. B asking her children questions (How are things in California? ... Did you talk to Kevin today? Can he accommodate us, do you think?

… Why don't you have another roll, aren't they *delicious*?) while Clifford passive-aggressively criticized their answers (I would think anywhere was great, if I had nothing but free time and money … Kevin can be tough on people he doesn't respect … Yes, have another, why don't you put some extra butter on it this time). It was awkward to the point of making me cringe here and there, but at least I could stay out of it.

Until Mrs. B made her way around to me.

"Min*er*va!" she chirped, startling me so much I almost dropped my fork, which would have been quite the boon for Plant, since there was a large bite of beef on it. "Such a lovely name. Don't you think it's a *lovely* name?" As this question appeared to be directed at nobody in particular, nobody answered. "Tell us all about teaching. You must have some funny stories."

Drat. "I … um …" I stalled with a sip of wine. *Funny* was not the first word that came to mind, when it came to my stories.

"What did you teach?" Tristan asked.

"High school," said Clifford. I had no idea why he was answering for me, but the way he said it definitely made high school sound like the clear underachiever path.

"History," I added.

"History!" said Mrs. B. "Here in North Carolina?"

"Yes, ma'am."

"Then you must already know a bit about the family, and Tybryd."

I laughed, more from relief than anything. This was

much safer ground. "I think I gave Snick a run for his money during our tour earlier."

Mrs. B glowed at me, and I might have launched into a monologue about Alistair Baird, and Tybryd, and the Gilded Age in general, just to keep on the subject. But Elaine had to go and ruin it by asking when I'd stopped teaching.

Double drat. I cleared my throat. "A while back. A couple of years." I knew how this went, and what came next: *Did you quit?*

And then: *Why?*

I drank some more wine—maybe more of a gulp this time—and looked down at my plate.

Slightly-lower-than-the-food-but-still-pretty-highlight: Percy riding to my rescue, like the knight he was named after. Maybe he noticed me stiffen. Maybe he was just good at reading people. I didn't know why he did it, but I could tell it was intentional.

What I didn't know at the time was just how far under the bus he was throwing himself, by changing the subject to one he knew his family wouldn't be able to resist. Or how fast that bus was going. Although I was about to get a pretty good idea.

"So!" he boomed, drowning out Elaine and startling Saltie and Bitts. "Paisley called me today—to tell me how much she's looking forward to the ball."

"Oh!" Mrs B looked surprised, then delighted. "Paisley is coming! But I thought you two broke up!"

"We did," Percy said, and despite having no idea who Paisley was, I nodded my agreement. Of course they'd broken up. How could you possibly tolerate being *Percy and Paisley*? It sounded like a seventies band.

Percy leaned back and narrowed his eyes at his father. "Which is why I didn't invite her."

"I thought the ball would be the perfect occasion to announce your engagement." Clifford refilled his wine glass—for the third time, by my count—and raised it to his son.

Elaine gaped at Percy. "You *didn't*."

"Of course I didn't." Percy made a *well, duh* sort of face at her. "Paisley and I are not engaged."

"In that case," Tristan said solemnly, "I think it would be a mistake to announce it at the ball."

"I invited her parents, too," Clifford said. In a completely normal tone, as if Percy didn't look like he was about to throw his steak knife into somebody's eyeball. "I got them a suite at Tybryd. Thought we might all spend some time together."

"Have you completely lost your mind?" Percy set down his wine glass a little too hard, splashing some very nice cab on my sleeve. He didn't seem to notice.

Clifford gave him a bland look. "For someone so eager to take control of the business when I retire, you certainly aren't doing much to earn it."

"You can't honestly expect him to sacrifice himself at the altar!" said Elaine. I noticed she'd gone a bit white, which seemed odd, considering it was Percy's future they were discussing. Maybe she just really loved her brother. Although they didn't seem to get along especially well.

Across from me, Tristan mouthed soundlessly, *Save yourself*. He flicked his fingers. *Run*.

I almost laughed, in that uncontrollable way you do when things are super uncomfortable, but somebody does something funny at the same time. I had to cough into my napkin to cover it. Thankfully, nobody paid either of us any mind.

"Sacrifice!" Clifford said with a snort. "As if marrying Paisley Grant would be a sacrifice. Have you *seen* Paisley?"

"Yes, but have you *heard* Paisley?" Tristan murmured.

Unlike his brother, Percy was clearly finding no humor in the situation. "This isn't the twelfth century, Dad. We don't do arranged marriages anymore."

"But we do mergers, right?" Clifford offered his son that same hearty smile he'd given me after he kicked my dog. "That's still something we do?" He winked at Elaine. "Shame the Grants don't have a son your age, isn't it?"

Without another word, Percy got up and walked out.

Chapter Three

Later that night, Snick took me down to the kitchen—in the basement, just like Tybryd's—to introduce me to the third member of our humble servant *(staff)* trio, the family's personal chef. Although there were day maids and landscapers and such, we were the only three who lived in the mansion.

Given the kind of homey meal she'd made, I was expecting a roly-poly little grandma type. That prediction was way off, as my predictions could be. (Especially when it came to what people would be like. Or what they would do.) There was nothing matronly about Rebecca. I'd have pegged her at about fifty, although her possibly prematurely white bob muddied my evaluation. She was slim and plainly energetic, her face angular, her chin pointed. I thought she looked kind of like an elf.

She invited us to join her at the farm-style table, where she'd been drinking tea from an old-fashioned china cup. The cavernous kitchen was a confusion of eras, its black-and-white tile floors and art deco touches mingling with state-of-the-art appliances and an original nineteenth-century fireplace. A large flat-screen monitor on one wall displayed, among other information, a list of rooms in a grid of green boxes.

"That's the modern equivalent of the old bell system," Snick explained. "They light up red if someone pushes the call button." He took his phone from his pocket, tapped the screen, then held it out to show me. "We have an app, too. We'll get you set up tomorrow."

Plant flopped down under the table, exhausted from his evening with Tristan's dogs, while I offered to make more tea. Rebecca resumed her seat at the table, directing me to the supplies and supervising me closely over the rim of her cup. I felt like I was under the watchful eye of a stern nun. Which was an odd fancy to have, considering I had not gone to Catholic school, and had never met any nuns.

"So, you had dinner with the family." She arched one perfectly groomed brow. "What did you think?"

"Oh, it was delicious!" I assured her.

But Rebecca was not one to require assurance. "I meant of *them*, ninny."

Had she just called me a *ninny*? Maybe I'd misheard. I set Snick's tea down in front of him, then took the seat across from her. "They seem nice, for the most part."

Snick, well, snickered. "For the most part."

"How diplomatic of you." Rebecca's light laugh ended abruptly with the smashing of her lips into a thin line of disapproval. "What is *that*?"

I looked down at the three perfectly innocuous pieces of saltwater taffy I'd transferred from my pocket to the table. You'd have thought they were used tissues, the way she was looking at them. "Banana taffy. I take it you don't want a piece? I might have some grape upstairs."

Rebecca inhaled through her nose, still glaring at the candy. "No. Thank you."

"Snick?"

He shook his head. He didn't look nearly as scandalized as Rebecca, but his brows had taken a definite downturn. "*Why* do you have taffy?"

"I always have taffy." I gave him a sage nod, as if that were the best piece of life advice he would ever get. Which, frankly, it ought to have at least been in contention for. A person *should* always have taffy. "And anyway, you need something sweet with tea. It's practically a rule."

"Cake, though!" Snick said. "Like, *tea cakes*? Or cookies. Maybe pie. Never, ever taffy. What are you, nine?"

"You're just wrong." I popped the piece I'd just unwrapped into my mouth, then kept talking in a deliberate display of bad manners. The sort a nine-year-old might have. "Ish iz shoft, fluffy goodness. Ish like eating a cloud."

"Well." Rebecca took a prim sip from her cup, clearly struggling to rise above it all. "I have some perfectly appropriate shortbread, but given your dubious palate, I take it that won't be necessary."

Snick raised his hand. "I wouldn't mind some shortbr—"

He was interrupted by a crash above us. It startled me so much I spilled my tea, and Plant raised his head, growling low. Before I could even grab a paper towel to clean up my mess, the crash was followed by a long string of shouts. Mostly muffled, but loud enough to pick out a few words that made my manners with the taffy seem elegant. Clifford, I thought.

Plant growled again. I stared at the ceiling. "What is going on?"

"One of the reasons we like to sit in the kitchen instead of the staff lounge," said Snick. "Entertainment." Apparently unfazed by the ruckus, he got up to get his own shortbread from a jar at the end of the nearest marble counter. When he sat back down again, he pointed upward. "That's Cliff's office. He holds most of his fights there."

Rebecca narrowed her eyes at the ceiling. "I don't hear anyone yelling back at him, though. So it's not Tristan." She glanced at me and added, "He's the only one who ever yells back. The other ones barely even talk back."

"You only say that because you never met Gwen." Snick cocked his head at the softer, calmer—but still clearly angry—voice answering Clifford's latest roar. "That's definitely Percy."

"Hang on," I said. "I'm still stuck on *holds most of his fights there*. Clifford fights a lot?"

"Oh, yeah." Snick drew out the *yeah* before taking a big gulp of tea.

"That's weird." I fidgeted with my taffy wrapper, folding it over itself. I wasn't as comfortable with confrontation as these two seemed to be. "I really didn't take Clifford for a yeller."

Snick shrugged. "His first line of attack is always to laugh and good-old-boy you straight to perdition. But woe unto you if you resist for too long, and he loses his temper instead."

"Once that temper's lost, it is *lost*," Rebecca added.

"Maybe that's what Percy was trying to avoid at dinner," I said. "He got really mad at Clifford, but he just got up and left."

"Mhm." Rebecca nodded. "He wouldn't fight in front of his mother. Or you either, probably."

"Then you know what they're fighting about." Snick leaned forward, eyes alight. "Spill it."

I bit my lip. On the one hand, I didn't want to gossip. On the other, I very much wanted to gossip. "Somebody named Paisley. Percy's ex, I gather? Clifford invited her to the ball, Percy didn't want her there. And then it got weird."

"Weird how?" asked Rebecca.

"Well, Clifford sort of ... *ordered* Percy to propose to her." I gave the tabletop a little smack with my palm. "Propose *marriage*! He was friendly about it, almost like he was teasing, but even I could tell there was some kind of threat behind it."

Snick drummed his fingers against the side of his cup, looking at Rebecca. "Think he'll do it?"

Rebecca grimaced. "I hope not. I cannot abide that girl. She wants agave nectar in everything."

"Who is she?" I asked.

"Paisley Grant." Snick took one look at my blank face and added, "The family that owns the Blissful Living Hotel Group. A bunch of brands fall under their umbrella, mostly five-star, hotel-slash-spa type things."

"Ah, so Clifford wants to make a deal with them for Tybryd, and he's hoping for a family merger." I frowned. "Now that I think of it, he did actually use that word, *merger*."

"Yes, and the stakes are high for Percy," said Rebecca. "The Tybryd Estate is a corporation, but Clifford owns something like ninety-five percent of it. And he's made it clear that he intends to keep that concentration of power in the family."

"That *same* concentration," Snick added. "As in, he's only going to pass those tasty shares on to one of his kids, to take over the whole business. Tristan doesn't want it, not when there's enough generational wealth in the family to guarantee no Baird *has* to work. And Gwen's out of the picture. So."

"So that leaves Percy and Elaine," I said.

Snick nodded. "And they both want it *bad*."

"Bad enough to marry somebody they don't want to marry, just to please him?" I asked.

"I guess we'll see," said Snick. "But yeah, my money's on a wedding."

Something above us shattered. Rebecca's eyes drifted upward as she took a calm sip of her tea. "I might put equal odds on a funeral."

∽

I'D LIKE to tell you something insightful about the morning I officially started working at Baird House. It would make me sound smart, or at least observant, if I could. But I can't.

I can tell you that I had some amazing overnight oatmeal for breakfast, courtesy of Rebecca. With nuts and dried cherries and this sort of cinnamony swirl. Did I mention it was amazing? Because it was. Funny, how well I remember that. But not the important things.

I can tell you that Clifford had a lunch meeting, and that it wasn't on his calendar. And that when I mentioned it wasn't on his calendar, he "joked" that I might like to get myself a dictionary and learn the difference between an assistant and a nanny, although he could see why I might get the two confused, on account of his youthful good looks.

I can tell you that he left the house wearing scruffy clothes and expensive but worn boots. I thought it an odd choice for a lunch, but he said he might go "up for a walk" afterward. I later learned that this was how he always referred to the hiking trails scattered throughout the area.

And that's about all I can tell you about that morning.

Except that it was the last time I ever saw Clifford Baird.

Chapter Four

I WAS the first one to realize that Clifford Baird was missing. Not in the *Oh, maybe he forgot to call* kind of way, or even the *Oh, maybe he's off on a bender* kind of way, but in the *Oh, maybe he got abducted or murdered* kind of way. His family was slower to catch on. Willfully, or otherwise.

Not that it didn't take me a while, too. After he went out for his mysterious lunch, I worked alone on a long list of ball-related tasks, plus a few extra requests from Mrs. B and Elaine. (The latter's hair needs seemed to be very complicated, and involved no less than four separate appointments, two of which required me to convince the stylist to make a house call.) That kept me plenty occupied, and it was all pretty self-explanatory, so I had no reason to call or text Clifford.

Nor did I suspect it was unusual when he never came back that afternoon. Tybryd was only a mile down the road, after all, and he had an office in the executive building (once a guest house) on the hotel grounds.

I had dinner with Snick and Rebecca in the kitchen, and didn't see Clifford that night, either. But that was no different from any of the other assorted Bairds. I heard them occasionally, or passed one in the hallway, but unless they needed something we weren't exactly hanging out. Despite the friendly (sort of) family dinner the night before, it quickly became clear that we staff kept mainly to ourselves.

By the next morning, Clifford's continued absence started to feel weird. I could still wave it away—but only just. It seemed odd that he would have me start in the middle of all the ball chaos, and then just leave me to my own devices. I'd had the impression he would be working from the home office most of that week.

But I'd already learned to my sorrow that his meetings weren't always on his calendar. Maybe he'd had an early one, and left the house before I got downstairs. Anyway, I wasn't so fond of our conversations to date that I wanted to pester him and force one, at least not until I had to.

Half an hour later, I had to. I needed a catering invoice, and it wasn't in the files they'd given me, paper or electronic. First I texted Clifford—no reply. Then I called him—straight to voicemail.

"Odsbodikins," I said to Plant. "What is that man doing?"

Plant went right on napping in the sun spot on the rug near the window, showing no concern at all for either my frustration or Clifford's whereabouts. I assured him he needn't trouble himself with getting up, and went off in search of the first Baird I could find.

Which happened to be Tristan, sweatpants-clad and yawning, starting up the main staircase with his Frenchies dancing around his feet (which seemed dangerous). Judging by his very unfashionable boots and the four leashes in his hand, they'd just come in from outside.

His eyes looked like they were sitting on top of a pair of puffy, dark moons, but they brightened when he saw me. "Hey! Where's Plant?"

"Napping in the office." I bent down to greet Saltie and Bitts, who had each chosen one of my ankles to rub their heads against. It was always strange, looking at small dogs, when I was so used to my big blockhead. They were just so … small.

"But he was up earlier," Tristan said. "He got up with you, right? And you must take him outside first thing?"

"Right …" I straightened back up to meet those tired eyes. I suspected I knew where this was going.

He gave me a pleading look. "It's just, these four delinquents get me up so *early*."

"You'd like me to walk them for you?"

"Just in the morning! Just long enough for them to do some business. Since you're going out anyway. They're no trouble at all."

"You just called them delinquents."

"*Affectionately.*" Tristan waved his hand in a way I guessed was meant to be reassuring, but that had the opposite effect, given one of the leashes he sent whipping around almost smacked me in the face. What was it with Bairds and hitting me in the face? "The way you'd call a big guy 'Tiny,' or whatever. They're amazingly good on leash."

The smile I gave him was mostly sincere. I was an assistant, after all. The title didn't leave much room for getting around the fact that it was my job to offer assistance. Besides, I liked Tristan. He'd made me laugh at that awful dinner. "I'd be happy to."

He patted my shoulder. "I'd offer to put in a good word for you with my father, but that's as likely to make him dock your pay as raise it. I could toss a few extra bucks your way, though."

"No need, that's what I'm here for. Speaking of your father, have you seen him today?"

"No, and I hope that trend will continue for a few more hours." Tristan snapped his fingers at the dogs, who to their credit, went to heel in a relatively orderly fashion. "We're going back to bed. But I saw my mom wandering the halls upstairs. Come and ask her for whatever you need."

I hesitated. Snick had told me that the family's living level was mostly off limits to staff. I wasn't sure a catering invoice warranted an emergency exception. "I don't want to disturb her."

Tristan rolled his eyes and shifted into a surprisingly accurate impression of his mother's voice. "But she *loves* you! You *know* she does! It's obvious in *every word*!" Ignoring my disapproving look—I supposed if pressed, he would have insisted it was *affectionate* mockery—he gestured for me to follow him. "She's not going to mind."

I left Tristan at the hallway that led to his room, and found Mrs. B in the gallery. She was standing very still, eyes fixed on the photograph from the first Baird costume ball. I came up beside her, tilting my head as I followed her gaze. Alistair and Emily Baird both held their masks to one side, the only pair in the crowd whose faces were exposed. It should have been a playful pose, but they didn't look playful at all.

"He was handsome, Alistair Baird, don't you think?" I said. "A little stern, though."

Mrs. B nodded absently. There was no exclamation of welcome. She'd barely even glanced at me as I walked up. "As was his wife," she said.

"Handsome, or stern?"

"Both, I guess. But I was thinking stern."

"She looks it," I agreed with a nod. "So, I'm sorry to disturb you, but I haven't seen Clifford all morning. I got down to the office at 7:30, and he never came. Do you by chance know where he is? Or maybe you can help me. I'm looking for a catering invoice ..." I trailed off as she exhaled a serrated breath. "I'm sorry, is something wrong?"

Instead of answering, Mrs. B nodded back at the photo. "Maybe *strict* is a better word than *stern*, for Emily. She gave no quarter. Not to her husband, and not to any outsider who tried to tarnish his reputation."

I had no idea what she was on about. Was she trying to draw some sort of parallel? Was I the outsider, trying to tarnish Clifford's reputation? This really wasn't the Mrs. B I knew, and I wasn't sure what to do with the new one. She seemed brittle—like the wrong answer might break her.

Well, if she wanted to talk about Emily, I guessed I'd talk about Emily. "That's interesting, that she wanted to protect his reputation. Percy mentioned the other night that Alistair was a bit of a womanizer, but there's no hint of that in any of the biographies I've read. Would that be Emily's influence? Could she have kept it that quiet?"

"Oh, certainly," said Mrs. B. "Emily knew how to control the narrative. Along with everything else. She was much better at all of this than I am."

"I'm sure that's not true."

"Better at navigating being a Baird wife, I mean. She didn't tolerate his infidelity, you know, if she found out about it. She cleaned up the mess, sure, but that didn't mean she was on his *side*. She punished him."

I laughed, if a little nervously. Nothing about this conversation seemed especially funny. "Punished him how?"

"Oh, little things." Mrs. B shrugged. "Depriving him of something he was looking forward to, or getting rid of something he loved. She sold his favorite horse once, in a pique. He was devoted to that horse." She smiled, still looking at Emily. "Not unlike how Clifford punishes people, actually. So I guess that came down through Emily."

I didn't know how to respond to that, so I let it be and went with, "You seem to know a lot about her."

More than that, she sounded like she *knew* her. I wondered if there were private letters, or something of that nature, that she might let me look at. As a history person, I couldn't help but be curious. From a purely academic standpoint, you understand; it only counts as gossip if it happened within the last fifty years or so.

"My mother-in-law was a great keeper of family lore." Mrs. B glanced at me, but only for an instant before turning back to the photo. "Clifford never came home last night," she said abruptly. A little impatiently, as if I'd been browbeating her. "Or at least, he never came to bed. Which probably means he's got a new mistress. Maybe she can tell you where to find him."

Needless to say, I felt awful. And awkward as all blazes. "I ... I'm sorry."

"Why? Are you his mistress?"

I stared at her. "Of course not."

She laughed, looking more like herself. I hoped that meant she was pulling out of the gloomy mood Clifford —and I—had put her in. "I'm sorry," she said, "I was teasing you, and it was in very poor taste. I told you Emily was better at this. But then, people *respected* her. Everyone just assumes *I'm* an idiot."

"Nobody assumes any such thing!" I protested.

"Oh, but they do." She wagged a finger at me. "If a woman is the least bit effervescent, people will mistake it for vapidness. You should be aware of that. And wary of it."

I swallowed. "All right. I appreciate the advice." I didn't, particularly, but thanking her seemed the polite thing.

Mrs. B smiled again. "Hold on, I think Clifford's

laptop is in our sitting room. I'll go and grab it for you. That invoice is probably on it somewhere."

The invoice, and what else? There might be all kinds of things on Clifford's personal laptop. A tiny (but maybe a tad bigger than I ought to admit without shame) part of me was already considering doing a little nosing around.

A mistress, huh? And who might that be? Percy had mentioned other assistants. Or maybe somebody who worked at Tybryd?

I waited until Mrs B came back down the hallway, carrying a slim computer under her arm. "Here. He thinks I don't know the password, but it's *Bairds-Gr84Life!*, which was *not* that hard to figure out, knowing him as I do." She spelled that out for me while I tried not to laugh, either at the password or this revelation that I wasn't the only snoop in the house.

Back in the office, my own snooping started out innocently enough. I found the invoice. Then, when Clifford didn't return my second text, I opened his calendar. Maybe he had a private one that he hadn't shared with me.

No such luck. But there was an email icon. So tempting.

I tried Clifford again, and again was bounced straight to voicemail. Obviously his phone was off. Maybe so his wife couldn't use it to find his location?

The man was in the middle of preparing for what was, apparently, the biggest event of the year for him. So big that one of his kids came home for nearly a month to help with it. (Although my keen instincts told me that Tristan was probably not all that helpful.) Yet he'd been gone for what would soon be a full twenty-four hours, had told nobody where to find him, and left no means to contact him. It was weird, wasn't it?

It seemed weird.

I decided weird was sufficient justification.

I opened his email. I didn't go so far as to read every single message, but I skimmed. Just the inbox. Quickly. More of a glance than anything, really.

I was still looking, guiltily, ears open for anybody coming to catch me, when I heard a voice I recognized in the hall. I chose not to think about *why* I recognized it, two days after meeting him, and having had only one real conversation with him. I just called Percy's name.

He poked his head into the office. "Hey, Mini Bigs, how's it going?"

I hoped by ignoring it, I could prevent that Mini Bigs thing from catching on. "I don't know, actually. Did you just come from Tybryd?"

"Yeah." Percy laughed as Plant's tail started thumping dramatically against the floor. He—the man, not the dog—crossed the room and knelt to rub his—the dog's, not the man's—belly. "Not going to get up, though, I notice. Lazy bum." Unbothered by this criticism, Plant rolled onto his back to offer greater access.

"He's not a morning person," I said. "Was your father there, by any chance?"

"No, he's not a morning person either. I thought he was working here all day."

"He left for a lunch meeting yesterday, he didn't say with whom, and nobody seems to have seen him since." I bit my lip. "I should apologize. I think I upset your mother when I asked her about it. She said he never came home last night."

Percy's face hardened. "Well then, the answer seems pretty obvious, no?"

"But if he's got a thing for, you know, dallying—"

"What an adorable word for a not adorable thing."

"—wouldn't he be better at it than this? I mean, not calling, turning his phone off, not lining up any excuses. That seems like amateur hour, doesn't it?"

"He doesn't care enough to bother making excuses anymore." Percy stood and rubbed his brows with one hand, like he was fighting off a headache. Was I the headache? "Let it lie. Or at least, do not bring it up with my mother again."

So yes, then. I was the headache. "I wouldn't," I assured him.

"If you need to play detective, you can come and see me."

I raised my brows. "Yes, I'm finding that very effective."

Percy tossed his hands. "What do you want me to say? I can see why this seems strange to you, but you're new here. Give it a few hours before we call the cops, the press, and the National Guard, okay?"

"Fine."

Well, it was sort of fine. Percy left, and I did not call anybody. But I did go back to Clifford's laptop. And open up his web browser. And check the search history.

Among several variations on his own name and Tybryd and, I'm sorry to say, unsavory search terms of a naughty nature, were three very interesting queries. Or one query, maybe, worded three different ways:

what rights does biological child have to estate
can a will be contested if children are left out
can disinherited blood relative sue for part of estate

I was about to take a screenshot and email it to myself, when I realized that Clifford, or anybody who looked at his laptop, would be able to tell I'd done it. So like any reasonable person, I took a picture of the screen with my phone instead. Then I sat back in the chair, unwrapping a piece of taffy and staring at the screen.

It wasn't especially shocking that Clifford Baird had questions about disinheriting his children. I'd personally heard him make veiled threats along those lines to Percy the night I arrived, and I had the impression he'd already written Gwen out of his will. And if he was so into having affairs, there could have been other kids that I (and maybe Mrs. B) didn't know about. This could have been about any, or all, of them. The shocking part was that he would ask the internet instead of one of the many high-priced lawyers he surely had to choose from.

Unless he didn't trust the lawyers? Or didn't want to involve even them in some secret goings-on? But if it was that much of a secret, you would think a person would know enough to clear his search history.

On the other hand, the person in question was not young, and oldbodies weren't generally celebrated for their technical proficiency. It was possible he didn't even know what a search history was.

I had a lot of questions, and finally, I stopped being the only one. By lunchtime, Percy was starting to agree that Clifford's continued silence was weird. By mid-afternoon, even Tristan was worried.

By evening, Elaine was telling her mother to call the police.

Chapter Five

"As I understand it, you had an altercation with Mr. Baird the day you arrived? That was Monday?"

Ruby Walker wore cat-eye glasses in teal plastic frames that stood out in all their neon glory against her rich brown skin. Neither her hair, cropped close to her head, nor even her perfect cheekbones could compete for attention. Those glasses were almost hypnotizing. It had taken me less than five minutes to realize she used them more as a weapon than as a vision aid.

If she was listening carefully, she took them off, all the better to sweep them back on when she wanted to let you know she was done listening—probably because you were being a nitwit, or at the least, disappointing. Her favorite move was inclining her head so she could look at you over the top of them, making you squirm under the weight of her disapproval.

This woman was clearly taking no sass from anybody. Which I supposed was part of the job; she was Bryd Hollow's chief of police. Apparently when the head of the family that founded and still owned most of the town went missing, you went straight to the top to solve the problem.

I had assumed, when she called me into Clifford's office, that she wanted to talk to me about Mr. Baird's activities and demeanor the day before. And I definitely wanted to talk to her about what I'd found on his laptop. I felt a lot less guilty for snooping, now that there seemed to be a good reason for it. I wasn't being nosy, I was being helpful! To the police!

But Ruby didn't seem to see it as all that helpful. She nodded. She wrote it all down. She took her glasses off and put them back on again. She assured me that they'd already taken his laptop, and that they'd be looking into it. Which probably meant she would have found the search history herself, so I guessed I was back to being a dirty snoop.

And then she started asking me whether I'd had an *altercation* with Clifford Baird.

I should not have been surprised by this line of questioning. A new person comes into the house, and then there's a disappearance almost immediately afterward? I wasn't just a suspect; I was a big one. Maybe even *the* suspect.

Odsbodikins.

I leaned back against Clifford's big desk, gripping its edge behind my back, where Ruby wouldn't see my knuckles go white. She hadn't sat, so neither had I. "I wouldn't call it an altercation," I said.

"But he hit you in the face?"

My hand drifted to my nose of its own accord. "A door hit me in the face. It was an accident."

Ruby made a noncommittal noise, then looked around until her eyes found Plant, curled up quite harmlessly in what had already become his favorite spot underneath the window. She let her glasses slide low on her nose, and for several seconds regarded him over the top of them. "And it was during this accident that your dog attacked him?"

I huffed. She could suspect me all she wanted, if she felt that was what it took to be good at her job. But there was no reason to go after poor Plant. "That's when my dog *growled*, and Clifford kicked him."

"So he assaulted your dog, rather than the other way around. That must have made you mad, huh?"

I gaped at her. "Odsbodikins, what did Snick tell you?"

"Odds what?"

"It's just an expression."

"Not one I've heard. Snick told me pretty much exactly what you're telling me."

"But you're spinning it, to make me look bad."

"Am I?" Ruby scribbled something else on her notepad, which I was pretty sure was just for show. Who wrote things down by hand anymore? "So you chose to stay on as an employee after this incident. Or accident. Whichever."

"Of course I did, why wouldn't I? It was an *accident*."

"I don't know, sounds like the dog kicking part was intentional." Ruby leaned forward and said, in a just-between-us-girls kind of tone that did not fool me one bit, "Clifford's a jerk, am I right?"

I cleared my throat. "He seems a little challenging. But it's nothing I can't handle."

"I see."

"Not that I, you know, *handled* it," I hastened to add. "That's not what I meant. I just meant that I'm fine with him." I wanted to clear my throat, but I considered throat-clearing to be suspicious behavior. Instead my voice came out all scratchy, which probably wasn't any better. "And let's be real. I am the last person in this house who had any reason to hurt him. I need this job."

"You're assuming he's hurt."

"What? Oh." I crossed my arms. The lowlight of this conversation was definitely turning out to be my own nitwitted mouth, and I was starting to sweat. "I'm assuming something less than pleasant has happened. I guess we all are, at this point. I haven't known him very long, but I'm pretty sure he wouldn't just run away less than three weeks before his big ball. He seems really invested in it. Emotionally, I mean, not just financially."

"That he is," Ruby said with a snicker, but she was back to bad cop before I could even return the smile. "Well, thank you, Ms. Biggs. I'll be in touch if I need anything else."

"I really do need this job!" I blurted.

There went her glasses again, down her nose. "What?"

"I'm just saying. I only moved here two days ago. I was in ... I wasn't happy where I was. This is supposed to be my fresh start. I'm counting on it."

"Okay."

"And I'm alone. Well, except for Plant. But the only people I know here are an old high school boyfriend and the ones I've met in this house. It's not like I could get another job by just snapping my fingers. Or another place to live. Or even a temporary place to stay. The ex-boyfriend is married, and we're friendly and all, but it would be a little weird for me to move in with them, don't you think?"

"Okay," Ruby said again, this time drawing out the second syllable. She was starting to look a little uncomfortable now. Too many feelings, was my guess.

I tried to rein it in. "So I would have no motive to harm my employer. Just the opposite. Without Clifford, I'm not at all sure of my job here. Which, as I might have mentioned, I need."

"Ah." She offered me the smallest of smiles. "Well, there's no need for you to worry about leaving Bryd Hollow any time soon. I'll ask you not to until this matter is resolved."

On that note, Ruby left, and I flopped into the nearest chair, face in my hands, to berate myself. I got way too flummoxed when nervous. And the babbling. Definitely too much of the babbling.

While I unwrapped a piece of taffy to comfort myself, Plant trotted over and put his heavy head on my knee. I scratched absently at his ears.

I'd been too focused on Clifford, and the family, to do much practical thinking about my own situation. It hadn't occurred to me until the moment I said it to Ruby that my job here was insecure. Technically, I was the whole family's PA, but in my admittedly brief experience, I seemed to be mostly Clifford's. No Clifford, no job. No grand historical home. Nowhere to go.

Unless, I guessed, Ruby decided to throw me in jail. Some fresh start that would be. Maybe it was a historical jail.

Well. My claim to being the last person who wanted to hurt Clifford Baird had certainly been accurate. In fact, I had every reason to try to get him back.

Preferably as soon as possible.

Chapter Six

Mrs. B rallied considerably, and in short order.

Despite the fact that her husband had just been reported missing two days before, she was determined to go forward as normal with the ball. ("I'm sure Clifford is *fine*! What could possibly happen to *Clifford*? He would never want us to cancel the *ball*!") It seemed to soothe her, to carry on as if he were going to walk through the door at any minute with a perfectly reasonable explanation. And her kids were happy to go along with whatever made her feel better.

That left me with a lot to do, and not much time to do it. I certainly couldn't be trotting dogs around one—or even four—at a time. I walked Tristan's dogs each morning with Plant, all five together.

Which was how I came to be on the front lawn of Baird House, face down in the mud and covered in French bulldogs.

It had been raining on and off since the day I got there, and said lawn was very squishy. Plus there were all those leashes around my ankles. And okay fine, I wasn't the most graceful of people, even under the best of circumstances. Let's not point fingers. The point is, I fell.

So down I went, and I mean all the way down. Flat on my belly into wet grass and mud. Plant frantically licked my ears. Two of Tristan's dogs jumped on my back. One started nibbling my foot. I didn't know where Sweetie was, but she couldn't have gone far, given that her leash (I knew it was hers, because they were color-coded) was wound so tightly around my neck that I was in some danger of strangulation.

I was trying to untangle myself enough to stand when I heard it: a feminine laugh. A pretty obnoxious one, if I'm honest.

"Oh my gosh, what *happened* to you?"

I blew my hair out of my eyes and looked up at the supermodel standing at the edge of the drive. "I fell." My tone was maybe not as nice as it could have been. But then, laughing at me instead of offering to help was maybe not as polite as she could have been.

"That big dog knock you down?"

Of course she would blame the big dog. Who, I might add, had obeyed my command to sit and was now waiting like a perfect gentleman for me to get organized, while the four tastebuds ran in circles, knotting their leashes even more and barking their little heads off.

"The small ones, actually." I finally managed to get to my feet and pull the dogs into some semblance of order, while she went right on staring, more at the dogs than at me.

"Oh my gosh, are those *Tristan's* dogs?" The woman

—who still had not introduced herself—squealed. "Ohhhhhh hi! I didn't recognize you guys! I'm so happy to see you!" Despite this claim, I noted she made no move to pet them, or even get down to their level.

A fake dog person. Which is, obviously, the worst kind of person.

Look, it's not that I mind if a person doesn't like dogs. I mean, I don't get it, but of course I don't *mind* it. There's no rule that says you *have* to like them. But fakes of any kind are bad enough, and somebody who would fake loving an innocent creature who is more than prepared to love them back is just not a nice person. Plus, in my experience, fake dog people almost always do it to score points with somebody they want to date.

I was wondering just who this particular fake was, and just whom she was trying to score points with, when the answer came trotting out of the house and down the front steps, calling out "Paisley!" as he came.

Percy. Well, that explained a lot. I'd been warned repeatedly by both Snick and Rebecca that Paisley was a ratbag, although they'd not used that *exact* word.

"What are you doing h—" Percy started, but as soon as he saw me, he veered onto the grass instead, and immediately took three of the Frenchies' leashes from me. "What happened?"

"I fell."

"Are you all right?" He shot an irritated look down at the dogs, including Plant, who was already giving him a hard lean. But at least it seemed to encompass them all equally.

"I'm fine."

"Per-*ceee*!" Paisley, presumably unable to bear his attention being drawn away from her, launched herself at her boyfriend (or ex-boyfriend, or fiancé, depending on whose narrative you wanted to go with) and began peppering his face with kisses like a fake blonde machine gun.

I tried not to look disgusted. Percy was less successful. He pulled a face and stepped back, putting a two-dog shield between them.

Apparently at a loss for what to say, Percy nodded at me. "So you met Minerva, I guess. She's our new PA."

"We didn't get around to introductions," Paisley said. She poked out her bottom lip in sympathy when I held up my muddy hand, indicating that I couldn't shake. "Bless your heart. *Darling* name, by the way."

"Thank you."

"So, you're the assistant." She flashed a big set of perfectly white, perfectly straight teeth. "Have you tracked Clifford down yet?"

"Er ..." I glanced at Percy, who was scowling at Paisley.

"What?" Paisley pouted again. "We should all be making jokes, because I'll tell you what, this is not a serious situation. I refuse to believe anything bad's happened. It's a prank or something. He'll be back."

She maneuvered around the dogs to put a hand on Percy's chest. "Anyway, that's why I'm here. I came as soon as I heard. I knew Bessie would be an absolute *wreck*, and you and Tristan and Elaine would be zero help in the positivity department. I wanted to cheer her up."

She must have noticed that the hard line of Percy's

jaw was not softening at this speech, because she squeezed his arm and tried a course correction. "Nothing yet?"

"Actually, there are a couple of things," said Percy. "The big one being that they found his car. Not Ruby, somebody from the county sheriff."

"Where?" Paisley and I asked at once.

"The lot at the Adley Falls trailhead, at the far end of Tybryd's grounds."

I frowned, for more than one reason. The name *Adley Falls*—and the idea of Clifford being there—made me uneasy for some reason I couldn't place. And why was I getting this news at the same time as Paisley? I'd taken Percy at his word when he told me to come to him if I wanted to play detective, and we'd been talking about his missing father a lot. "You didn't tell me this."

"I just found out," he said. "Ruby called with an update."

"What," said Paisley, "and you didn't immediately report it to the PA? Did you tell the day maids, at least?" She laughed in that way a person does when they're not really joking. I'll confess I wanted to slap her, just a tiny bit. "Why don't they just track his phone?"

"They're working on it, but it's turned off," Percy said. "The second thing was that they confirmed he had lunch with Simone the day he disappeared. But he left the restaurant safe and sound, and she has an alibi for after. Client meeting, two or three witnesses."

"Who's Simone?" I asked.

"Simone Benoit, the last PA." He scratched the back

of his head. "Guess they must've had some unfinished business or something."

Ah. The ex-mistress, then. Or present mistress? One of the mistresses? I bit my lip, thinking about what this might mean. Nothing, I guessed, if she really had an alibi. Adley Falls, though ... that definitely meant something. "But I thought they already checked all the trail lots. I told Ruby on Wednesday that he'd mentioned maybe going hiking."

"They checked all his usual spots." Percy shrugged. "This just isn't one of them."

That made me even more uneasy, although I still couldn't have said what was bothering me about it. Not that I needed anything special to bother me about being at my new job for less than a week and my boss disappearing. And me being a suspect.

Paisley, on the other hand, was apparently not bothered at all. "But this is good news! Hopefully he took a fall and broke his leg or something."

Percy and I both stared at her.

"What?" she asked, and for all the heavens to witness, the woman actually stamped her foot. "I'm only saying, that would explain everything. At least it would mean he's not *dead*."

"Paisley," Percy said, mostly through his teeth. "Please make sure you don't use the word *dead* in front of my mother."

"Oh, I would never! And I will tell her exactly what I've been trying to tell you, which is that everything is going to work out fine!"

"Let's hope so," said Percy. "I asked Ruby if we could

get some civilians to help with the search, but she said to stay away so we don't spoil any tracks, or scents for the dogs. I don't know if leaving it to the pros is such a great idea though, there's miles of trails. It could take a long time—"

"Not that long." I swallowed (which was a shame, because I had a little bit of mud in my mouth) and nodded at the two cars coming up the long drive: one from the Bryd Hollow Police Department, and one from the county sheriff's office.

The pros in question had arrived.

Chapter Seven

WORD among the day maids was that Bryd Hollow was rife with *Cliff fell off a cliff* jokes.

Which was to be expected, I guessed, since Clifford Baird had, indeed, fallen off a cliff. Or at least, he'd come to be at the bottom of a cliff. Dead, if that wasn't clear.

They say everyone grieves in their own way, but to be perfectly frank about it, I didn't see a whole lot of grieving of any kind at Baird House. I mean, nobody was openly dancing or anything, but they all seemed more relieved than sad. It was like a more relaxed version of the house it had been the day I arrived. Even I relaxed, once Mrs. B assured me that I still had a job.

There was no formal, official reading of a will, at least not one that I was asked to attend, but maybe that only happened in movies. In real life, the Baird family lawyer showed up at the house practically in the wake of the police, and it only took Snick a matter of hours to ferret out that Percy and Elaine had inherited equal shares of the business. It seemed that pitting them against one another and forcing them to compete had been a purely manipulative exercise. Grand entertainment for a hornswaggler like Clifford Baird.

No wonder nobody missed him.

There wasn't much to tell about the scene of his death, at least not as far as the sheriff or Ruby were concerned. Slick trail, wet leaves, sheer drop over a waterfall. Lots of rocks. Nobody had any reason to suspect that Clifford would commit suicide, so the whole thing was about as straightforward as the death of a missing person could be. Everybody knew it was an accident.

Everybody except me.

Because Adley Falls was still ringing a not-very-nice bell in my head. And because I finally, the day after Clifford's body was found, figured out why.

The waterfall was one of a dozen small ones in the area, the hiking trail one of many more than that, and neither was notable as far as the search engines were concerned. I didn't find anything more than a poorly scanned trail map. I wasn't surprised; me being me, if I'd come across the name of an obscure little trail I'd never seen, it was almost certainly someplace a lot older than the internet.

Despite all the stress and flurry of planning my new boss's funeral, which I think we can all agree is not the ideal way to start a new job, I carved out a little time after dinner to explore the Baird House library. There were a lot of old books in there (a lot of books, period), and I thought surely some of them would cover a bit of local history. Maybe I could find something that would jog my memory.

Mrs. B had already given me permission to use the library whenever I liked. Still, I couldn't help but be furtive. I felt like a governess in a gothic novel, snooping where she shouldn't before her employer inevitably clubs her over the head. Plant seemed to agree this was a danger, and opted for my nice cozy bed upstairs over coming with me.

The room was all dark wood and soft leather, with looming built-in shelves interrupted only by the fireplace and the floor-to-ceiling window on the north wall. The latter offered a lovely mountain view, but northern exposure made for soft light, a disadvantage that was offset by an assortment of lamps, both standing and table, each with an odder and more garish shade than the last.

It smelled wonderful, like paper and applewood smoke. One of many things I appreciated about Baird House: there were a lot of fireplaces, and none of them had been converted to gas. (Although at first I'd been a little horrified at the waste of so much wood, until Percy happened to volunteer, unprompted, that it was all sustainably sourced. As were the cheaper softwoods they used at Tybryd. Environmentally friendly improvements seemed to be a pet project of his.)

The shelving system, if it could even be called a system, seemed a little haphazard. But eventually I found a more-or-less cohesive history section, covering a wide range of geographies and eras. I worked my way up, pulling over the wheeled ladder when the shelves got too high for me to reach. The oldest books were at the very top, presumably to keep them away from grubby hands like mine.

And I mean *old*. All of them were faded and weathered. A few had no titles: small, plain, unassuming volumes that might have been journals. Feeling a familiar thrill at the possibility of a primary source, I wiped my hands on my jeans just to make sure they were not actually grubby.

I ran my fingers along the row of spines, scanning titles and authors where I could see them, but stopped short when I felt something incongruous—fake leather. In fact, I was pretty sure it was *plastic*. The book, blandly titled *Machinery Of The Modern Age*, was only made to look worn, right down to the fading *M's* in the script, and the faint—and fake—thumbprint near the bottom.

"Well, well," I whispered as I pulled it from the shelf. "What are we hiding here?"

As I suspected, it was one of those fake books that's actually a box. I flipped open the flimsy cover to find a stack of cash neatly secured with a piece of plastic wrap around the middle, a cell phone, and two folded, yellowed pages that turned out to be torn from a naughty magazine. (*Ew*. Also, *why*?)

It was the phone that interested me—mainly because I recognized it. Plain black, and not a smartphone. A burner, no doubt, but even for a prepaid phone, it was practically an antique. In other words, it wasn't the sort of thing you saw very often.

But I'd seen it quite recently: in Clifford Baird's hand, the day he kicked my dog.

This was the phone he'd been using when he walked out of the gym room. I was sure of it; I could *see* it. How had I failed to notice (consciously, anyway) at the time that he was using such a weird phone?

I reminded myself, in my own defense, that I had just been hit in the face.

I put the rest of the stuff back and replaced the fake book on the shelf, then checked the call history on the phone. It looked like it had only been used to call one number. Which I promptly dialed.

A recorded voice thanked me for calling JoraLab, and informed me that it was after business hours, but that if I knew my party's extension, I could enter it to leave a message.

It's worth noting here that I was still on the ladder, leaned against the top shelf, as I did all of this. Before coming to Baird House, I'd never actually seen one of those library ladders in person. But I knew from movies that they were notoriously unreliable, particularly if one were a young woman (perhaps a gothic governess) at a point in a story where one needed to be caught by a hero —or a villain.

You'd think that would have put me on my guard.

It did not. Or maybe it did, but the phone had me distracted enough to let my guard down. Either way, when Percy and Tristan came barreling into the room, laughing despite their fresh loss, with four happy Frenchies trailing behind them, I was startled.

I jumped. The ladder wobbled. I started to slide.

Percy stepped forward, as if to catch me if the worst should happen, while Tristan stepped back, as if to make sure I didn't fall on him.

As fate would have it, I did not fall. But I did drop the phone.

"Drat!" I jumped off the ladder to get it, but Percy beat me to it. *Double drat.*

Fortunately for me, he barely glanced at it as he handed it to me; he seemed a lot more concerned about whether I'd hurt myself. He certainly didn't seem to recognize it.

I tucked it into my back pocket before either Baird brother could get a good look at it, and started talking way too fast. Babbling, you might say. "Sorry. Did you need the room? I was just ... there's a history section there. Your mother told me it was okay to come in here. I think there are some journals up top, I was just trying to see—"

"Right, because you have that history thing." Percy had already moved around me to climb the ladder himself. "I think it's Emily's journals up here. Want me to grab them for you?"

"Emily *Baird's*?" I blinked at him. "And you're going to let me have them, just like that? You're not mad?"

He handed down three of the leather-bound journals I'd spotted earlier. "Why would I be mad?"

"I don't know. I just thought you Bairds were protective of your family secrets."

"Family secrets?" Percy laughed as he hopped back down. "Tristan, did you put an insane wife in the attic again?"

"Not me," said Tristan. "I'm not the marrying kind." He grinned at his brother. "And neither are you, it would seem, judging by how mad Paisley looked when she left."

You'd think Paisley leaving would be good news, but I was sure it just meant she'd gone back to the resort, where she'd taken a room. I had no doubt she would be back for the funeral. And probably to boss me around some more before that. She seemed certain she needed to "help" with the arrangements, and that poor Mrs. B would never survive the ordeal without her.

"I meant more along the lines of Alistair's attic wives," I said to Percy. "That night at dinner, when I first came, you told me he was a womanizer, and then asked me not to tell anybody."

He shoved his hands into his pockets, looking a little hurt. "Minerva, there is nothing more annoying than a person who can't tell when you're being funny."

"That was you being funny?" I coughed to hide a laugh. "I mean, you know, you're funny so *often*. Sometimes it's hard to keep up."

Percy narrowed his eyes at me. "You're quite the comedian yourself. We should go on the road." He nodded at the books, now tucked safely under my arm. "Knock yourself out. Just, you know, be careful with them. My mother would kill me if they were damaged."

"Can't have that." Tristan clapped Percy's back. "We're down a man as it is."

See what I mean, about them not grieving? I supposed Tristan's snark could have been a coping mechanism. But it still seemed awfully odd, making offhand jokes about his father's death before the man's body was even buried. Even Percy cringed.

But I had bigger things to think about than Tristan's lack of respect for the dead. Like what business Clifford had with JoraLab that was so secret, he needed to conduct it with a burner phone.

∽

I'D BEEN LOOKING for Adley Falls in the wrong place. The answer wasn't in the history or the geography of the area. I should have been looking for a biography.

It came to me, as stubborn memories so often do, when I stopped trying to remember, and focused on something else.

Alistair Baird, founder of the Baird dynasty, captain of industry and builder of Tybryd, husband to the woman whose journals were tucked away in my nightstand drawer, had fallen to his death over Adley Falls.

Exactly as, more than a century later, his great-grandson would.

And nobody had yet mentioned this? I could see the general public not knowing the exact trail where Alistair met his end, but surely at least some of the family knew, right? If I knew, if I'd read the name *Adley* in some half-forgotten corner of a cobwebby book someplace, then it was open—if obscure—knowledge. Alistair's own blood must have known.

More importantly, what did it mean, the two Bairds dying not only in the same way, but in the same place? I could not view it (or anything, really, which was both a highlight and a lowlight of my character) as a coincidence.

It was a carriwitchet I could not fathom. I would certainly be thinking it over, and scrutinizing Emily

Baird's journals for whatever I could learn about her husband's death.

But at the moment, I was way too busy freaking out about JoraLab.

So I shoved the thing about Alistair firmly to the back of my mind, and kept scrolling. It was maybe half an hour since I'd left the library; I was sitting on the couch in the staff lounge, Plant draped over my lap and snoring, while I stared at my phone's browser and waited for Snick to come up for the night. I needed somebody to talk things over with.

My reflex, even after only knowing him a short time, would have been to talk to Percy. But I was getting a sinking feeling that it would be unwise to trust any Baird, at least for the time being.

Snick, on the other hand, was above suspicion as far as I was concerned. He had no reason to push Clifford off the side of a mountain, apart from sheer irritation with the man. If anything, planning a funeral right up against the ball was only causing more work for the both of us. And speaking of unnecessary work, hatching up a murder plot was no easy thing. I couldn't see Snick bothering with it.

Besides, we worked closely together, and I remembered him being around the afternoon Clifford had disappeared. I couldn't attest to specific times, but that was still more than I could say for any of Baird House's other residents.

So when he finally trudged up the stairs, I hissed his name and gestured dramatically for him to come and sit with me.

He pouted. "I'm tired."

"It's for gossip."

"Well in that case." He plopped down beside me on the couch, causing Plant to heave a put-upon sigh and get down on the floor.

I held my phone in front of Snick's nose.

"JoraLab," he said, squinting at the screen. Then his brows shot up. "Paternity testing. And is this gossip about you?"

"Of course not." I smacked his shoulder. "It's about Clifford."

"What, you think one of Clifford's kids isn't really his kid?" Snick snorted. "Mrs. B would never."

"Did you know that home paternity tests can't be used in court?" I asked. "I just found that out. You have to go to a lab."

"Interesting tidbit. Is it going anywhere?"

I pulled the burner phone out of my pocket to give him a quick look, then as I replaced it told him how it had been hidden, how Clifford had been talking on it the day I came, and how JoraLab's was the only number in the call history. When even that pile of evidence failed to impress him, I told him how Alistair Baird had died.

Snick only shrugged. "What has that got to do with anything?"

"I don't know yet, but this can't all be coincidence." I unwrapped a piece of taffy, then started ticking off the not-coincidences on my fingers. "Clifford was searching the internet to find out whether a disinherited biological child can contest a will. He had a secret phone for calling JoraLab, which does, among other things, paternity testing. And then he died in the exact same way as his great-grandfather. Who was, incidentally, also a womanizer."

"Okay, so you think Clifford was murdered. I guess by one of his kids he was trying to disinherit?" Snick shook his head. "That makes no sense. He already disinherited Gwen. He knew it was possible."

"Unless he was afraid it wouldn't hold up in court," I said. "Where is Gwen, exactly?"

Snick waved at that. "In Italy, living in bliss with her strapping Italian husband and her beautiful Italian children."

I chewed at my thumbnail until inspiration struck. "Simone, then. What if she was pregnant?"

"Then keeping Clifford alive to pay child support would seem like her best option."

"Okay, so Mrs. B. Maybe she didn't want another heir to the throne."

Snick gave me a look that suggested my detecting skills were not up to his standards. "Can you really see tiny Mrs. B pushing a guy like Clifford over the side of a mountain?"

"No," I admitted, then tossed my hands. "I don't know. I don't have all the answers, but I can tell you for sure there are questions. I'm taking that phone to Ruby first thing tomorrow."

The county sheriff's office had turned the investigation into Clifford's death, such as it was, over to the Bryd Hollow Police. His car had been found on county land, but the precise location of his last breath was almost certainly on Tybryd property, which made it town jurisdiction.

"Tomorrow?" Snick groaned. "Must you? I suppose you expect me to cover for you."

"It won't take that long, I'll—" I stopped abruptly. "Did you hear that?"

Snick clearly hadn't, but Plant's ears perked up, assuring me that the creaking floorboard I'd just heard was not my imagination. Nobody had come up the stairs while I was in the lounge. Had somebody been lurking up here this whole time?

I got up and stalked into the long hallway that led to our rooms, ready to confront the eavesdropper. Rebecca was there, leaning against her open doorway, face in her phone.

"Rebecca? I didn't know you were up here."

"Came up right after dinner," she said, thumbs furiously working at, I supposed, a text. "Had a headache. Just woke up, needed a drink."

I nodded, a little let down that I wasn't about to catch a spy in the act, and thereby unveil a murderer. Her story probably checked out; she looked disheveled enough to have been napping. (And disheveled was not Rebecca's usual state.) Plus her door *had* been closed when I came up, and none of us kept them closed normally, when we weren't in our rooms. I'd been too preoccupied to give it much thought at the time.

She finally looked up, rolling her eyes, and started walking back toward the lounge, where we had a little dorm-style fridge stocked with water and iced tea. "Except my sister interrupted me. She keeps bugging me for gossip about Clifford. I keep telling her it was just an accident."

I followed her. "Do you think that's true?"

"What, that it was an accident?" Rebecca shot me a confused glance over her shoulder. "That's what we've been told, so I assume so. I can't see Clifford doing it on *purpose*, can you?"

No, Clifford Baird definitely did not strike me as the sort of man to commit suicide. But if Rebecca's list of ways to die only included *accident* and *suicide*, it had a pretty glaring omission on it.

She greeted Snick, gave Plant a pat, got her bottle of water from the fridge, and went back to her room. None of these were lurking behaviors. And I supposed I couldn't really accuse Rebecca of lurking in her own room. It wasn't her fault I hadn't known she was up there.

Besides, what exactly was I suspecting her of? Killing Clifford? It seemed unlikely that the paternity situation had anything to do with her; she was probably too old to be Clifford's long-lost daughter, and definitely too old to be his pregnant mistress. So what motive would she have had? Had he insulted her beurre blanc or something? (Well, probably. But that was nothing to how he'd treated his family.)

I was being silly. Overly suspicious. You might even use the word paranoid, and it wouldn't be entirely misplaced.

But really, when you've just realized you might be sharing a house with an unknown murderer, that's kind of a smart thing to be.

Chapter Eight

WHEN I SAID I was going to bring that burner phone to Ruby "first thing," what I actually meant was "as soon as I finished walking the dogs, paying a stack of bills connected to the funeral, and arguing with Snick about whether or not it was okay for me to leave for a little while." So fourth thing, really.

It was Sunday, which should have been my day off, but that didn't matter when there was a funeral happening on Tuesday. Not to mention the ball hurtling at us like a runaway train, just ten days after the Bairds were to bury Clifford in the family plot at Bryd Hollow's famous St. Asaph's church.

Mrs. B was every bit as determined to go forward with the ball as ever. If anything, she'd have liked to move up the date, so the people flying in for the funeral could just stay. Thank heavens we employees (with a fair amount of help from Percy) managed to talk her out of that.

All by way of saying, by the time I got upstairs to gather my things and go, it was mid-morning.

And the phone was gone.

Emily's journals were still there in the nightstand drawer, but the phone I'd tucked in behind them was nowhere to be found. "Odsbodikins," I whispered, then narrowed my eyes at Plant. "Useless mutt. If you were a hound, you could track it down for me."

Plant thumped his tail against the bed, but I was pretty sure that was just because he could tell I was going somewhere, and was hoping I'd bring him with me. I was still on the fence on that one. On the one hand, I doubted he'd be welcome at the police station. On the other, it was unseasonably cool for so early in September, and he'd do just fine waiting in the car. He did so love being invited along.

I cast one more angry glance down at the empty space where the phone ought to have been, then slammed the drawer shut. It seemed all but certain now that Clifford had been murdered—and that I was sleeping under the same roof as his murderer. Why would somebody want to stop me from taking evidence to Ruby, unless they were afraid it would implicate them?

Percy and Tristan were the obvious suspects; apart from Snick, they were the only two who'd seen the phone. I hadn't thought either of them *saw* saw it, but it certainly wouldn't have been the first time I was wrong in life.

As for Snick, he'd been in my sight nearly all morning, plus all the reasons I already had for being sure he was no more guilty than I was. Including an alibi that I could attest to personally for much of the day Clifford died. He was probably the only one in the house I could afford to clear as a suspect, unless I wanted to count Plant.

But none of that meant that either Percy or Tristan was *definitely* the guilty party. There was Rebecca. How much had she overheard the night before? Granted, I could think of no motive for her, and lots of motives for the Baird family, but she certainly had opportunity.

Even Elaine and Mrs. B weren't entirely above suspicion. Either of them could have peeked into the library and watched me find that phone; I'd left the door open.

When it came down to it, any one of them could have done it. Or even all of them, conspiring together, like a Christie novel. Really, who wouldn't want to give Clifford Baird a shove?

"Okay Plant," I said, "you're definitely coming with me. I can't just leave you here, surrounded by any number of murderers."

We were in the car fifteen minutes later, and it was a glorious feeling, being free and on our own. It was a gorgeous day. September is usually a summer month in North Carolina, even in the mountains. But this was full-on fall, clear and crisp in a way that always gave Plant (and me) extra energy. Plus, it was just nice to be driving; I hadn't even seen my car in the week since I arrived.

The week since I arrived. I pulled a piece of taffy out of its wrapper with my teeth, then shook my head in disbelief. Had it really only been a week? Actually no, it hadn't. Six days. I was just six days away from my old life. It seemed so distant already.

"Well, you asked for a new one," I muttered. "Put that in the be-careful-what-you-wish-for basket."

I was still going to see Ruby. Sure, I had nothing to show her. And I was a suspect myself. This might even make things worse for me.

Even so, I couldn't just not tell her. Withholding evidence was a definite crime, wasn't it? Not that I had any evidence to withhold. But surely I had a duty to tell her what I knew.

Besides, I really wanted to get out of Baird House for a little while, and a meeting with the police chief was the only excuse for leaving that Snick was prepared to accept.

But I will allow that the missing phone made the visit feel a tad less urgent. There was something else I wanted to see first. Despite the fact that the clock (well, Snick's clock) was ticking on my time away, when I left Baird House's long drive I didn't turn right toward town, but left toward Tybryd—and the Adley Falls trail.

The resort was a close neighbor to Baird House, but I didn't stop there, instead following the road when it bent away from the grand entrance. For today, I would have to settle for a distant glimpse of the red roof, the same as Baird House's, and the top of the famous ferris wheel they kept running year-round beside the main building.

The entrance to the trail Clifford had walked that fateful day was still police-taped. Which was kind of odd, considering everyone was calling his death an accident, but I guessed when somebody as important as Clifford Baird died, you didn't shut the book on it right away. A quick internet search earlier that morning had told me that there was another trail below, along the wide stream the falls (and Bairds, it would seem) fell into. The walk would take Plant and me onto Tybryd's land, which I assumed was fine if you weren't a guest but were a Baird employee.

It didn't take long to walk from the little parking area to as close as we could get to the falls. Which wasn't all that close—the area around where Clifford's body had been found was cordoned off, too. It didn't matter; it was close enough to hear the roar, and see the water tumbling down in the distance.

I'd just wanted to see it. I couldn't really have said why. It wasn't as if Alistair Baird's ghost was going to be there, waiting to explain everything to me. As for Clifford Baird's ghost, I was pretty sure I didn't want to meet him, not even for an explanation.

Plant had more practical concerns. Like getting as wet and smelly as possible, as quickly as possible. Naturally this involved jumping into the stream. And since I wasn't the type to flout the local leash law, also dragging me into the stream.

It wasn't more than knee deep in the part he splashed over to, but there was nevertheless much sputtering and threatening on my part. Which only made Plant dance around, certain we were playing. Which in turn only got more water all over me. Including in my nose. That brisk day I was talking about? Not as nice when you're soaked in it.

"Plant!" I yelled as best I could through a cough. "Sit down *right now*!"

I'd gotten Plant for protection; he'd had training. But as you might have spotted, he was maybe the littlest bit lacking in discipline. (Which is really to say that I was lacking in disciplinary skills. Or maybe disciplinary will.) And he was absolutely convinced that everything was a game. The *right now* command, never overused and always spoken in my very harshest voice, was my last resort when it came to signaling that he was supposed to be working.

It got the job done. Plant immediately dropped his goofy dog smile and sat, right there in the stream, water flowing all around him from a little cluster of rocks nearby.

He was closer to the bank than I was, so I went to him. I wagged my finger at him as I stalked over, launching into a lecture about learning to tell the difference between *fun play time* and *serious investigation time*. He listened, head tilting to one side and then the other, but he didn't look especially repentant.

When I got closer, he stood and gave an enormous shake, dousing me a second time. I turned my head to avoid yet more water in my nose, and a glint of silvery light among the rocks caught my eye. Something smallish and metal was stuck between them.

I bent to pick it up and discovered that it was a flask, the little kind people keep in their jacket pockets. It was freezing from the water. I tugged my sleeve over my hand (which only helped a little, since my sleeve was also pretty cold) and held the flask up for a closer inspection.

I didn't open it. But I did find a set of initials engraved on one side.

C.G.B

THE SMART THING TO do would have been to abort the mission and go home. I had a towel in my car, which was helpful for my hair and skin, but of limited use to my soaked jeans. Plus, I smelled like a wet dog. This was no shape to be going to see the police chief in.

But I'd already lost one piece of evidence at Baird House. I wasn't about to risk losing another. While I had that flask firmly in my possession and under my eye, I was going to deliver it to Ruby. Dog stench or no dog stench.

Plant thoroughly agreed, mostly because I told him we were going for a ride.

Although I was pretty knowledgable in the area of Bryd Hollow history, my only direct experience with the town was driving through it on my way to Baird House the day I moved in. I hadn't had much chance to explore, but as I turned onto Honor Avenue, I saw pretty much what I'd expected to see.

Much like the Bryd Hollow of yore, the current version existed mainly in support of Tybryd. In this era, that meant serving as a quaint destination for the strolling, shopping, spending tourists. Most of the shops had cutesy names, and all had the same gray stone faces, a pretty contrast to the red brick of the sidewalks. Each of the old-fashioned lampposts had a strange black rhombus at its base, the purpose of which was a mystery to me until I got out of my car at the corner of Honor and Purity.

They turned out to be speakers, pumping out oldies for the pedestrians, swing and early rock-and-roll. The era made sense; this modern Bryd Hollow had been born in the fifties, around the time Tybryd became a resort. But all day, every day? I guessed they were going for an All-American Small-Town Paradise kind of thing, but to be honest, it was a little unsettling. I felt like I was on a movie set. Or in a Stephen King novel.

I left Plant in the car with an open window and a rubber toy stuffed with a few treats, and headed past the town hall (picturesque clock tower and all) to the police station. I hoped Ruby would be there on a Sunday, but even if she wasn't, the flask would be safer in the hands of whatever officer I left it with than in a drawer in my room. Apparently.

The officer behind the front desk (by which I mean, the closest of the three desks in the room) did not seem impressed with the disheveled stranger inquiring after Ruby. Ruby, when she poked her head out her office door, looked equally sour. Could she smell me from there? It was possible. The station was tiny.

"It's all right, Roark," she told the officer, before giving me a short nod. "You can come back."

Her office was small and homey, with bookshelves and pictures and a scented candle on her desk. Not what I'd expected from Ruby, who'd struck me as cold. The look she gave me was cold enough, though, when I started to sit down. I guessed she objected to me dousing her chair with wet-dog-smelling stream water. I settled into an awkward sideways lean against the wall instead, careful that only my shoulder came into contact with it, and not my jeans.

Oddly enough, my monologue about phones and

flasks and the history of Adley Falls appeared to do nothing to increase Ruby's enthusiasm for my visit.

"Can anyone else confirm the existence of this prepaid phone?" she asked, when I finally shut up.

"Other than the person who took it, you mean?" I raised a brow, but Ruby's face suggested the retort wasn't as cute or clever as I thought it was. I shrugged. "Snick. Possibly Percy or Tristan."

"But none of them actually saw the call history."

"Not while I had it, no."

"And even if we could find this phone, you have no certain way of knowing it was Clifford's." Despite the fact that she was sitting and I was standing, Ruby somehow managed to look down at me over the top of her teal-framed glasses. "That's kind of the point of these phones."

"But I saw him using it," I said.

"Can you prove it was the same phone?"

"I guess I can't *prove*—"

"Can anybody else corroborate what you saw?"

I bit my lip and shook my head. "Snick didn't remember one way or the other."

"So the phone is meaningless." Ruby held up her hands when I started to protest. "I'm not saying you're lying. Only that it doesn't matter. I can't use a phantom phone as evidence."

"My testimony wouldn't be good enough?"

She didn't respond to that. "I'll confirm the flask is Clifford's, and if it is, things like that phone are a moot point. If he'd been drinking, that supports his fall being an accident. I have no evidence at all that any crime has been committed here."

"But you'll send the flask to the lab, or whatever?" I asked. "You'll find out what was in it? What if it was poisoned?"

She didn't answer that, either. Only gave me another disapproving look that would have put the strictest of schoolmarms to shame. (And I would know, having been a schoolmarm myself, once.) "I assure you, Ms. Biggs, I'm doing my job, and you can expect me to continue to do my job."

"Of course! I know. I didn't mean to suggest otherwise. I'm just a concerned member of the household, is all." Even as I said it, I realized I could lean into that a little harder. "Mrs. B hasn't been able to come down here herself, but she'll want to know what I found out."

All of that was true; she was overwhelmed, and of course she'd want to know about all this. Not that I had any plans to tell her. "What about the other thing I told you about?" I asked. "Did you know that Clifford died in the same spot where Alistair Baird died in 1913?"

Ruby slowly twirled a pencil between her fingers like a baton. "As a matter of fact, I did. My grandfather used to tell me stories about Adley Falls being haunted. There are probably a handful of people in town, old ones mostly, who would know old Alistair died there. But I highly doubt it's common knowledge."

"Not common knowledge," I repeated, pointing at her. "Meaning if somebody pushed him off that same spot, they might assume nobody would notice the coincidence, and it would be taken as an accident."

She pursed her lips. "Meaning it's unlikely to be related. It's a treacherous spot on a slippery trail. Alistair wasn't the only other person to die there, you know. Someone fell from the top of that trail in 1927. Drunk"—she nodded at the flask on her desk, which she still hadn't bagged or anything—"like Clifford, maybe. They put up a guard rail after that, but I guess it rotted or something, because someone else fell in 1953, and that time it was a little kid. At that point the county was more than happy to rid itself of the liability. They sold the land to the Bairds cheap."

I frowned, taken aback by that last bit. "I thought it was Tybryd property all along."

Ruby shook her head. "George—Alistair's son—sold it to the county at one point, but his son Richard bought it back in 1954, the same year they converted the estate into a resort."

I cocked my head. "You seem to know a lot about this off the top of your head."

"I told you I already knew Alistair died there. I looked up the rest as soon as I remembered that."

"Which means you were investigating!" I said, feeling I'd scored several points. "Because you suspect it wasn't an accident, too."

"I was investigating," Ruby said blandly, "because that's kind of what I do."

So no points for me, then. "And in the course of this investigation, you never found his phone?"

"Nope. Probably lost in the water somewhere, but we'll keep looking, for the sake of thoroughness."

"And no footprints or anything?" I pressed.

Ruby snorted. "Plenty of footprints. Clifford Baird was not the only person who used that trail."

"You just said it was dangerous."

"It is, if you're dumb enough to go near the edge at the top, but if you're not dumb, it's a nice hike. There are fewer people this time of year, with the rain and the mud, and it being a little early for leaf-peepers. But it's not like it was completely abandoned."

"Yet there were no witnesses who saw him fall." I narrowed my eyes at her. "And no signs of a struggle?"

"None," said Ruby. "Do you need reminding that I don't work for you?"

"Of course not, I'm sorry, I'm only—" I began, but she cut me off.

"—asking on behalf of the Bairds. So you said. Which is why, as a courtesy, I've been happy to tell you as much as I have. But I don't work for them, either." She gave me another stern look. "Clifford fell, Minerva, and his family has been through enough. I see no reason for you to upset them further."

I almost laughed at that. "They're holding up okay."

To my surprise, Ruby's mouth twitched a little in return. "Be that as it may." She stood, a clear indication that she'd had enough of me.

Which was fine, because I felt about the same. Plant never minded waiting in the car, but even he had his limits. And my socks were really wet. "Thank you. I appreciate you taking the time."

"You're very welcome. And you can tell Bessie the medical examiner worked through the weekend. He expects to release the body to the funeral home tomorrow."

I already had my hand on the door handle, but I turned around at that. "The medical examiner? You did an autopsy, even though you're so sure it was an accident?"

"He died in the water. An autopsy is always performed in cases of an unwitnessed drowning." Ruby crossed her arms. "But I would think as Bessie's assistant you would know she requested one, anyway. She wants the whole works, tox screen and everything. Those results will take a little longer, but I've already informed her of that."

"Right. Thanks again." I left quickly, and took Plant to Noah's Bark afterward for a new toy, to make up for leaving him so long. On any other day it would have been a treat to meet the pet shop's eponymous beagle, and the owner of both shop and dog, a woman named Gretchen with a cotton-candy cloud of white hair, who looked roughly 293 years old. Both were charming, but I was too distracted to pay much attention to them. Not even Plant licking my ear all the way home could take my mind off Mrs. B.

She'd specifically asked for an autopsy—even though it turned out they were going to do one anyway. And a tox screen. Interesting. Maybe she genuinely wanted to be sure the investigation was as thorough as possible. Or maybe the lady was protesting too much.

In either case, I clearly wasn't the only one who suspected—or knew—that Clifford Baird had been murdered.

Chapter Nine

Paisley Grant was working my very last nerve.

I had no idea why she was even still there. Not that she was *there* there; she was still staying at the resort. But for somebody who wasn't there, she was awfully present. Ever-present, in fact.

She would have said she was there because she *loved* Mrs. B, and just because she and Percy were in an "off period," that didn't mean she stopped loving his *family*, and anyway it was *obvious* that Mrs. B needed her. I know this because that's exactly what she did say. Many, many times.

I saw little indication of any of these things, except for she and Percy being off. I supposed whether it was an off period or an off forever remained to be seen. Meanwhile, Mrs. B seemed to have plenty of people around to help her, without Paisley having to be underfoot.

And anyway, to be perfectly honest about it, Mrs. B seemed more together and confident than she had when her husband was alive. If you asked me, Paisley was just trying to sink her claws in anywhere she could, now that her only real ally in the family was gone.

The only highlight of that was that it made her pretty much the only person I could mentally rule out as a suspect in pushing Clifford off the cliff. The rest of her being there was fully and entirely lowlight.

Her idea of helping consisted mainly of following me around all day, making ridiculous suggestions and then asking me if I was writing them down. Could we get a string quartet for the reception at the house after the funeral? (No.) What about something for the kids, maybe a bounce house? (No.) Shouldn't we have a theme? *(No.)* I couldn't help but wonder whether she wasn't projecting some of her would-be wedding plans onto this funeral. If so, Percy was lucky he got out when he did. A sentiment he seemed to heartily share.

The afternoon before the funeral, Plant and I were walking through the first floor with Mrs. B and Paisley, taking note of Paisley's many complaints about how things had been set up. "You really ought to tell your people to move that credenza!" she said to Mrs. B, in the same urgent tone she might have taken had the credenza been on fire. "Someone is going to set a drink down on it, see if they don't!"

Mrs. B pressed a fist to her sternum and grimaced, though not, apparently, because she shared Paisley's concerns about the furniture. "That salad we had for lunch was a bit *acidy*, wasn't it? *Delicious*. But *acidy*."

"Heartburn?" Paisley gave Mrs. B what I'd quickly come to recognize as her signature pout. "You're just under so much *stress*. Maybe you should go take a nap. I can handle the rest of—"

"I'll go see if Rebecca has some heartburn pills in the kitchen," I offered, maybe a little more loudly and quickly than was polite. I was praying I could eradicate this problem quickly enough to avert such drastic action as putting Paisley in charge. And why was that even an option? Why were none of the other Bairds at their mother's side?

Tristan was probably napping himself, under a mountain of Frenchies. And Gwen wasn't coming home at all, which I understood from Snick had been a sore blow to her mother. Pantry gossip held that Mrs. B had assumed that with Clifford gone, the whole rift would be automatically mended. But not only was Gwen busy with her own family across an entire ocean, she still held a grudge against Mrs. B for not taking her side more actively when the fight with Clifford went down.

But Elaine or Percy, surely, should have been around to help. Most especially the latter. It was *his* ex-whatever plaguing this house and everyone in it. He should have been the one pretending to write down all her nitwitted ideas.

"No, don't ask *Rebecca*!" Mrs. B said. "I don't want her to know her salad gave me *heartburn*! It would hurt her *feelings*! I have some Tagamet up in my room, I'll just go get those."

"*She* can go, can't she?" Paisley tossed her head at me.

"I sure can!" I chirped. I set down my tablet (the one I was pretending to write things down on) and slapped my thigh for Plant to follow me. Mrs. B called out her thanks as we fled.

By the time I was out of smelling range of the Italics Sisters' competing perfumes, I already felt infinitely better. Not only would I get a few blessed minutes away from Paisley, but I'd have an opportunity to look around the second floor—the master bedroom, no less—something I'd been short on excuses to do. The disposable phone might have been gone, but I was sure that Clifford's reason for using it was not. Somewhere in this house, there was something that would tell me what he'd been up to. And why it had gotten him killed.

I trotted up the grand staircase, Plant at my heels, and turned down the hallway toward the family's bedrooms. How long could I claim it took me to find Mrs. B's pills? Would I have time to look through Clifford's dresser? His nightstand? His medicine cabinet, for sure, assuming his and hers were in the same general area. They were always looking through medicine cabinets on the detective shows.

But Plant had other ideas. He put his nose on the floor, sniffed hard a few times, then made a beeline for Percy's mostly-but-not-entirely-closed door and pushed his way right on inside.

"Plant!" I hissed.

At the same time, I heard Percy say, "Hey, big guy!"

Odsbodikins.

I stopped short at his door, then knocked and peeked in. Percy was kneeling on the floor by the bed, scratching the sides of a very energetically wiggling Plant.

"I'm so sorry," I said. "We were on our way to your

mom's room for a Tagamet. I guess he just smelled you. I didn't know you were home."

Percy hit me with the dimples. "I told everyone I was going to Tybryd." He leaned forward and whispered, "I'm hiding."

I snickered. "From Paisley?"

"She's here?" He scowled. "Why?"

Because she's on a mission to make me truly understand why one human being would murder another. I cleared my throat. "I would think you're more qualified to answer that question than I am."

"I thought she was going to Lake Halpern for the day, or I'd have gone to rescue my mom. I'm not *that* much of a coward. I was just hiding from ..." He waved a hand vaguely.

"Well, pro tip: you might want to consider closing your door if you want to hide behind it."

"I thought I did. Come in and close it now, will you?"

"Uh. Sure." I didn't much like the idea of being shut up in Percy's room with him. Or maybe the problem was that I did like it. I definitely didn't like the idea of spending all my antacid-fetching time in here instead of rummaging through Clifford's things.

But I did as he asked, mostly because I was afraid it would look weird if I refused. And also because Plant, the snorting buffoon, was likely to give Percy away before much longer, and much as I'd bemoaned Percy leaving Paisley for the rest of us to deal with, I wasn't that mean. If Paisley had kissed me every time she saw me, I would have been hiding too. Although probably a little farther away. Spain, maybe.

Despite my living in close quarters with my employers, it was strange to be in one of their bedrooms. It might have been uncomfortably intimate, had Percy's not been so impersonal. Apart from a couple of photos on the dresser and nightstand, we could have been in a hotel. I wondered if it had always been like this, or if there had been a teenage phase with posters taped to the walls, or before that, toys littering the floor.

"You said Tagamet, right?" With one last scratch of Plant's head, Percy stood up. "I can grab you some."

But Plant wasn't willing to give him up so easily. He bounded after Percy into the bathroom. This was immediately followed by the sort of banging noise a thing makes when it hits a tile floor.

Knowing Plant, that something was likely to be a trashcan. "Plant!" I called, and followed my errant dog into Percy's bathroom, which felt even weirder than being in his bedroom.

Sure enough, I was greeted with the sight of an overturned trashcan, and Plant and Percy playing tug with a sock. An orange sock, I might add. Not pumpkin or rust or clay, but *orange* orange. Who owns orange socks?

"Plant!" I clapped my hands.

"My fault," Percy said with a laugh. "I threw these away this morning. He dove right for them."

"I wouldn't call throwing those away a fault."

He laughed again. "My mother has a thing for giving us weird socks. She thinks they're funny." Percy ceded control of the sock. Plant celebrated his victory by prancing around the spacious bathroom, holding his awful orange prize high.

"You shouldn't let him win, you'll only encourage him." I got down on my knees and righted the trashcan, then started picking up the mess, which was considerable. I guessed the maids hadn't emptied that can in quite a while. I only hoped I wouldn't be obliged to touch any used tissues.

I saw nothing gross, but I did see, amid a second pair of very ugly socks, a somewhat alarming assortment of, well, drugs. Old prescription bottles, ibuprofen bottles, thin cardboard boxes of various kinds. A few containers of sunscreen. I glanced at Percy, who by then had joined me on the floor.

Catching my look, he shrugged. "I cleaned out my medicine cabinet."

"Along with your sock drawer?"

"I had some extra time."

"Because you were hiding."

One side of his mouth quirked up. "Exactly. And I have a tendency to organize when I'm stressed. You want to get rid of expired stuff, you know." He leaned over to scratch Plant's head. "I did not foresee that I'd be exposing a dog to temptation and potential poisoning."

Plant poked Percy several times with the sock, in hopes of another game of tug. I glared at him—Plant, not Percy—as I tossed a few more things into the can. "Leave it."

He dropped his trophy, but not without resentment. Heaving a sigh, he flopped down on the floor, head between his paws.

I looked back at Percy. "I'm sorry. He just can't resist a sock."

"Don't worry about it." Trying, and failing, to look offhand about it, Percy grabbed an empty box out of my hand and tossed it into the can. But he wasn't quick enough, and I'd already seen the label: Dramamine. Which I knew from a lifetime of throwing up on airplanes was used for motion sickness.

His eyes slid away from mine. "I took Paisley for a ride on Tybryd's ferris wheel, to give my mom a break from her. You'd think I'd be used to it, but I still get sick every time."

I resisted the urge to ask whether he meant every time he rode the ferris wheel, or every time he was with Paisley. Feeling bad that I'd apparently embarrassed him (although I wasn't sure Dramamine properly qualified as an embarrassing drug), I stuck with the most innocuous of the debris after that. When everything was set to rights, Percy opened the medicine cabinet—which did, at a glance, look very neat and organized—and held out a box of Tagamet.

"Thank you," I said. "Sorry again for the disruption."

"You seem to be sorry a lot." He winked at me, repeating something I'd said to him the night we met. I generally cannot bear winking in a man, but on Percy it looked natural and kind of boyish and not smarmy at all. It was really starting to get inconvenient, how adorable he was.

His fingers grasped mine as I took the box. "You're not going to tell on me, are you?"

He had *such* nice hands. I laughed, but I pulled my

own hand away as quickly as I could without looking weird about it. "Certainly not. What do you take me for?" I smacked my thigh for Plant. "Let's go, you."

Percy followed us back through the bedroom. "Speaking of what I take you for, I found out a few things about you."

I tried to keep my voice casual. "Like what? I said let's go!" The last bit was for Plant, who had jumped onto Percy's bed and made himself comfortable on the admittedly inviting cloud of a duvet.

"Leave him be for a minute," Percy said with a wave. "This doesn't look like the kind of house where dogs are allowed on beds, but they always have been. I know, for example, that you taught high school until two years ago. Or two and a half now, I guess."

My casual voice took a slight turn towards tart. "Fizzing sleuthing, considering I told you that."

"And that you hate it when anybody brings that up. And you get that look on your face, like you have right now."

I looked down at the floor and crossed my arms. "What's your point?"

"I know why you quit. I know all about Natalie Jones."

My eyes snapped up to find that Percy's had drifted down, to the v-neck of my sweater. I knew it wasn't for licentious reasons. He was looking for a scar.

"Do you." It wasn't a question. I most certainly didn't want an answer. Natalie's name had brought on a little flare of panic that dragged my voice straight past tart and all the way to sharp.

Percy shoved his hands into his pockets and shrugged. "I just wanted you to know that I know, in case you ever want to talk about it. Being new here and all, and knowing so few people. Secrets can be lonely things."

Of course I didn't want to talk. Not about *it*, and not about the fact that I was such a coward I'd abandoned my fledgling teaching career not quite a full year after *it*. "You seem to know a lot," I said instead. "Mind if I ask how?"

"I had you checked out. After you hedged about it at dinner."

"I did not *hedge*. And checked out by whom? You mean like a private detective?" I put my hands on my hips. "You had me *investigated*?"

He rubbed the back of his neck. "I wouldn't say *investigated*. It was a simple background check, it's not like I had to call in Poirot to crack the case."

"Why Poirot and not Holmes?"

Percy blinked at me. "What?"

Not that I blamed him for being confused, by either the weird question, or the angry way in which I'd asked it. "I would think Sherlock Holmes would be the first detective that comes to mind for most people, when they want to make a famous detective reference. Are you an Agatha Christie fan?"

For some reason, this irritated me greatly. *I* was an Agatha Christie fan. Poirot was *my* favorite detective.

"I guess." The crease between Percy's brows when he looked baffled was cuter then I'd have liked. "I don't know why you're getting so mad. Is it not reasonable for me to do a background check on somebody we've brought to live with us?"

I huffed. "I think I'm the one who ought to be worried about living with you people, all things considered."

His face hardened. "Meaning what?"

"Meaning that I would think you'd have a better use for this detective of yours than wasting his time on me. Unless, of course, you've got a reason to keep him distracted from the real crimes going on around here."

It was a low blow, and it landed. Percy looked stricken. I felt a little guilty, especially since I did not actually think he'd shoved his father off a mountain. But like I said, Natalie's name had put me in a bit of a mood.

Natalie Jones had been disgruntled when I gave her son Jared a B in my class. It was the only B on his entire transcript, and she was convinced it was the reason he didn't get into his university of choice.

Funny, I couldn't even remember anymore what university that was. It didn't matter. He probably didn't want to go there nearly as badly as his mother wanted to have a son who went there. She'd probably already bought the stupid *Bragworthy University Mom* sticker for her car.

Most of the parents in that town could've shocked a lightning bolt and scared a psychotic clown with how competitive they were over what schools their kids got into. The result was an outrageous amount of pressure, which had a terrible effect on their children.

Not to mention the effect it had on me. Natalie had

dealt with her disappointment by shooting me twice in the chest.

I snapped my fingers. "Plant, come. Now." With great reluctance, Plant jumped off Percy's bed and came to me.

He looked back at Percy as we left the room, but I didn't.

Chapter Ten

Clifford Baird's funeral didn't really have a lowlight, which is probably a terrible thing to say about a funeral, but here we are. The highlight was a very close contest between the food, and the gossip.

"These are amazing." Paul stuffed another pastry filled with fig-and-shallot jam into his mouth and closed his eyes. "I kept telling you Rebecca was wasted at Tybryd."

"And I kept telling her the same," said Carrie.

"Rebecca came from Tybryd?" I asked.

"From a *junior* position at Tybryd." Carrie pressed her lips together, as if disappointed in Rebecca's lack of ambition. "She was way overqualified for it, but I guess she just wanted to get her foot in the door. Can you imagine? She had her own restaurant in Indiana or Ohio or wherever it was. The woman was made to rule over her own roost."

I cast a longing glance at a passing tray of champagne. "Get her foot in the door at Tybryd, specifically? That seems kind of random. Does she have family in Bryd Hollow or something?"

Carrie shook her head as she took a sip of her own drink. "She's friends with Tybryd's executive chef. I don't know how close, but he was the one who told me to hire her. And I guess they're still in touch, because I just saw her over there yesterday."

"Maybe he still mentors her," said Paul. "Maybe this is actually *his* fig-and-shallot jam." He pretended to clutch at some invisible pearls.

Carrie swatted him with a cocktail napkin. (A *chartreuse* cocktail napkin, thanks to Paisley's input. It was truly hideous.) "I think she just needed a change of scenery. I know she was taking care of her father for a long time, cancer or something, and then he died. Anyway, when the private chef position opened up here you can bet I called Simone and got her on the schedule for an interview."

My eyes drifted across the packed drawing room, and I noticed that Snick did not bother to long for the champagne; he just took a glass. We weren't supposed to be drinking. We almost certainly weren't even supposed to be in here with the guests. What kind of butler attends his boss's parties instead of presiding over them? But the funeral reception wasn't a party, exactly, and nobody had *specifically* forbidden us from paying our respects. By which I mean, from enjoying Rebecca's excellent food and a little well-earned time off.

I'd had the sense to leave Plant upstairs, at least. Big slobbery dogs seemed like a good place to draw the line, especially considering Clifford hadn't liked him much.

And anyway, not even Tristan's dogs were present, which was probably as much a blessing for them as for us.

"Speaking of Simone." Paul lowered his voice and elbowed me. "Did you hear she was the one who had lunch with Clifford the day he died, *and* that it got kind of heated? What do you think, any chance she ..." He made a little pushing motion with his hands, and a popping noise with his mouth.

"Really?" Carrie gave him an exasperated look. "At the man's funeral?"

I covered a laugh behind my hand. I'd mostly lost touch with Paul since high school (until I emailed him out of the blue to ask if his wife could get me a job), but back then he was the biggest gossip I'd ever met. It was comforting to see that some things never changed. "Simone has an alibi for the time of the murder, though."

"I already told him that." Carrie rolled her eyes at her husband. "He just likes stirring the pot."

"You heard that too?" I guessed word really did travel in a small town. Maybe Clifford's death was an accident, after all; it was hard to imagine anybody getting away with murder here without half of Bryd Hollow knowing about it fifteen minutes later.

"She hears everything," said Paul. "Ruby is Carrie's aunt."

"Oh!" Well, that explained it. I cocked my head at Carrie, surprised this hadn't come up before. "Now that you mention it, you do have the same supermodel cheekbones."

"A gift from my Grams," Carrie said. "She was a dead

ringer for Eartha Kitt. But between inside information from Aunt Ruby and inside information from Tybryd, you can see how Paul didn't marry me for my cheekbones."

"He does love his inside information," I agreed.

"A lot of good it's doing me this time." Paul sighed in mock dejection. "Ruby's still saying accident."

"Until she has a good reason to say otherwise," said Carrie. "But she is investigating still, so she's open to the possibility that it's more."

"*You* seem to think it's more," Paul said to me. "Any particular reason?"

Once again, I looked over the crowd in the drawing room. I knew the dining room was crowded too, and even part of the ballroom. Most of the staff from Tybryd were here, along with what must have been just about every resident of Bryd Hollow. I didn't know any of them, other than Carrie and Paul. But judging by the amount of nanty-narking going on, not one of them was sad.

I'd been focused on the Bairds, but seeing all these guests enjoying the refreshments and apparently having the grandest of times, I realized there could have been any number of people who wanted to see Clifford dead. He'd been a powerful man, and not a nice one.

I started to say as much to Paul, but I was interrupted by the arrival of Elaine, and the ensuing hush that fell over the room.

The hush shortly gave way to whispers. I couldn't work out what the problem was, other than that she was late. She'd been at the service, though, and at the graveyard. So what if she'd taken a little breather before coming back here for the reception? She was arm-in-arm with a guy I'd never seen before, but he didn't look especially shocking, either. Clean cut, handsome.

I looked to Paul for answers, but he was looking at Snick, who'd just sidled over to join us.

"Well, well." Snick put his hand to his chest and raised one of his pale brows at Paul.

Paul raised a brow back. I wondered if they had some sort of busybodies' secret handshake they'd do next. "Did you know?"

"Nope, not a clue." Snick studied Elaine and her (boy?)friend, who were now chatting with an elderly couple. Elaine and the friend looked relaxed and happy. The elderly couple, not so much. If you'll pardon the in-somewhat-poor-taste funeral joke, their smiles were stiff enough to be on the corpse's face.

"I'm willing to bet her parents didn't have a clue either," Snick went on. "Guess she has more game than I thought. Would you have thought it of her? I would *not* have thought it of her."

"Definitely not," said Paul. "She does not seem the type."

I'd quietly tried to get their attention several times during this exchange, to no avail. Finally I just shoved Snick's shoulder. "What's going on? Who is that she's with?"

Carrie shook her head at the men. "Nothing is going on, unless you're an incorrigible gossip. That's Phil Mendoza. He's a vet."

"Veteran, or veterinarian?" I asked. "Not that it matters. Neither seems particularly scandalous."

"Veterinarian," said Carrie. "And it's not scandalous at all. He's a very nice, normal, scandal-free person. Way too nice for her, actually."

"Now who's the gossip?" Paul grinned at her.

Snick made an impatient noise. "The point is, he's a *townie*. And not even a real doctor! Clifford would never have put up with it. Not even if they weren't serious, and if she's brought him here, I'm guessing they *are* serious."

Now all the raised brows and wagging tongues made sense. Elaine had been competing with Percy for control of the business—or at least she'd thought so. I didn't know her well, but I was pretty sure she never would have jeopardized that by being with somebody unsuitable. Especially not after what happened to her sister. Not to mention Clifford trying to arrange Percy's marriage.

And now she was so eager to go public with this guy, she couldn't even wait an hour after her father was in the ground to do it.

The only person who didn't look surprised, confused, or downright distressed was Tristan. I wondered if he knew what a terrible job that glass in his hand was doing of hiding his laughter.

Mrs. B approached her daughter and the vet. We were all on tenterhooks—even Carrie, I think, whatever she said—as we watched them. It had gotten so quiet again, I could hear them talking from the other side of the room.

Now that she was in front of her mother, Elaine looked as tense as the rest of us. "Mom, you know Phil."

"Of course I do." Mrs. B gave Phil a warm hug. "Thank you so much for coming, Phil."

"I'm sorry for your loss, Mrs. B."

"Thank you." Mrs. B wound her arm through his. "Come on, let's get you a drink."

And just like that, the budding scandal was squashed. Nobody should have been surprised. Clifford might have considered himself above the rabble of Bryd Hollow, but Percy had told me specifically that Mrs. B raised them not to put themselves above anybody. She could hardly be mad when Elaine took her upbringing to heart, could she?

No, now that Clifford was gone, the path for Elaine and Phil was entirely clear. All their problems had been tossed over Adley Falls, to be carried away by the stream below.

Like I said, there was an almost limitless number of people who wanted that man dead.

Chapter Eleven

THERE WAS a bee in my bonnet. One thing I believe, and have always believed: if you want to see forward, you have to look back. As a history person, naturally I suspected that the key to understanding Clifford Baird's death was understanding Alistair's. And if Clifford's hadn't been an accident, maybe Alistair's hadn't, either.

Sure, it was possible it was a stupid bee, in a stupid bonnet. But it was my bee, my bonnet. Since Ruby had no apparent interest in that line of investigation, it was up to me to find out how the deaths of the two Baird patriarchs were related.

Emily Baird was no help at all.

Or if she was, I couldn't figure out how. I couldn't find anything at all in those dratted journals. First, because not one single entry was dated. I didn't even know which of the three books came first, much less where to find the days surrounding Alistair's death. For all I knew, she wasn't even journaling at the time.

Second, because she'd evidently been very fond of

sketching. So much so that a lot of the entries were nothing but a sketch. And just because she'd been fond of it, that didn't make her good at it. A lot of them were completely indecipherable. (None of them, as far as I could tell, depicted a man falling over a waterfall.)

Third, because her writing was downright flighty. She would mention going into Bryd Hollow, or Newport, or New York, and then talk about a flower she'd seen there and nothing else. Or she would have lunch with her mother-in-law, and describe nothing but the china. Not what they talked about. Not even what they ate. The dowager Mrs. Baird seemed to have a lot of china.

This was not the stern, strong Emily who appeared in her photograph, and in Mrs B's stories about her. I thought of the steel in her eye, that ghost of a smile, and I couldn't reconcile the two Emily Bairds at all.

Plainly, one of them was not who she seemed. But which one?

A nitwit could not have faked that clever face. Whereas a clever person could fake being a nitwit.

The false Emily had to be the one in the journals. But diaries were meant to be private. Why fake yourself, for yourself?

Which led me to the obvious conclusion: the journals were written in some sort of code.

I'd like to say that this realization led to an immediate breakthrough, and that I quickly put to rest the mysteries of both men's deaths. But what it actually led to was a fair amount of frustration.

I stayed up late, in the nights following Clifford's

funeral, poring over Emily's words and drawings. But with the ball still looming on the horizon, I didn't have a lot of time to devote to cracking codes. And the lack of sleep was doing little to improve either my concentration or my enthusiasm.

But eventually, a pattern or two did begin to emerge.

Like how often Emily talked about flowers. It took me a while to notice, because she talked about a lot of things that seemed inconsequential, and not of the sort you'd bother to note in a journal. Plus, lots of people cared about flowers.

But the thing was, Emily Baird was rich. Really rich. She'd have no business doing actual *gardening*. Phrases like *How I despise roses* might make sense, but *I cut the roses today*? Why would she have been cutting her own roses?

Which was when it occurred to me that maybe the roses weren't flowers at all. Maybe none of the flowers were flowers.

Looking at the entries through that lens, matching up visits and events, it became clear to me that Alistair's mother's code name was *cornflower*. The china at Baird House, which Emily spoke of in fairly critical terms, had a cornflower pattern. And cornflowers were always present on holidays like Christmas, despite being entirely out of season at that time of year.

I was extremely proud of myself for putting all of that together. Until I realized it told me nothing whatsoever about Alistair Baird's death. Or, by extension, Clifford's.

To what was to turn out to be my (and several other

people's) considerable dismay, Ruby Walker had much better luck with modern technology than I did with history. She came to the house almost exactly a week after the funeral, just three days before the ball, looking decidedly grim. She wanted to speak with Mrs. B alone.

"Well you *can*, of course, if you *insist*," Mrs. B said. "But I'd really prefer for our assistant to join us, so she can take notes. I might forget something, and Percy or Elaine will ask about it later. You know how that always happens, like when you go to the doctor, and you come back and someone asks you a question, and you can't remember a *word* he said? It's maddening! Isn't it just maddening? And then whoever asked you the question is always so *annoyed*."

She could have just as easily recorded the conversation, but I didn't point that out. None of her kids were home, and Mrs. B had been leaning on me a lot (whenever she could get away from Paisley, who was staying in town until the ball). I suspected what she really wanted was for me to be with her, if Ruby had bad news.

Maybe Ruby got that same impression, because after giving me her usual inspection over the top of her glasses, she nodded and said that would be fine. Amid Mrs. B's exclamations of *Wonderful!* and *Thank you!* and *It's so nice to see you, by the way*, the three of us headed for the office, Plant at my heels as usual. The ladies took the pair of armchairs, while I got behind the desk with my laptop. Plant settled down at my feet with a sigh, as if Ruby had interrupted some fun plans he had.

"First, I need you to understand something," said

Ruby. "The body wasn't found straight off. That can compromise certain types of lab results."

Mrs. B glanced back at me and said, "Be sure you get that, won't you?" before turning back to Ruby. "What sorts of results do you mean?"

"Toxicology," Ruby said. "Here's what I can tell you. Clifford almost certainly had a few drinks before he went on the hike. Is that unusual behavior for him?"

"What, drinking?" Mrs. B snorted. "He had *lunch* before he went on the hike. It would have been much more unusual for him to have had a meal *without* drinking."

"Most hikers would know better than to get dehydrated ahead of time," Ruby pointed out. "Especially hikers who are, if you don't mind my saying, a little advanced in years."

Mrs. B waved this away. "Clifford was in excellent physical condition! He wouldn't have been worried about the *Adley Falls* trail."

"Why do you say that?" Ruby asked, and I was glad, because I had the same question. I hadn't been able to walk the actual trail, but I'd seen the area. It didn't look like an especially easy hike. Not to mention that Clifford wasn't the first person to take a fall there.

"That trail is more than a stroll," Ruby went on. "And it was wet at the time."

"I suppose it's a little steep in spots, but nothing *Clifford* couldn't handle!" Mrs. B said. "They used to bring *schoolchildren* up there for picnics, once upon a time, didn't they?"

I couldn't see Mrs. B's face from where I sat, but I

narrowed my eyes at the back of her head, pondering the question of how she knew that children used to go up there—yet apparently didn't know that one of them had died. Was she more familiar with the waterfall's morbid history than she was letting on?

If her mother-in-law had been, as Mrs. B had put it, such a keeper of family lore, wouldn't Mrs. B know who else had died up there, too? Yet no Baird had ever mentioned it, at least not in my presence.

Not that I mentioned it either. I did my best not to discuss Clifford's death with any of them, on account of them all being potential murderers who might smother me in my sleep.

"All right," Ruby said, but she pursed her lips. "What about dimenhydrinate?"

Mrs. B laughed. "I'm sorry, dime what?"

"Dimenhydrinate," Ruby repeated. "You might know it under the name Dramamine. It's most often used to prevent motion sickness."

I coughed, as if noise would somehow cover the fact that I'd just jumped so hard in my seat, I was surprised my head hadn't hit the ceiling.

Plant was convinced that any startle response of that magnitude was a sure indication of a spider. He jumped up, wiggle-wagging nervously as he nosed me and the desk in turn, ready to eat up the offender.

"Plant, it's fine!" I whispered, desperate for him to stop drawing attention to us. "We're fine."

It was too late. Both ladies were staring at us now. I cleared my throat again and said, "Um, sorry. Spider. I'm scared of them."

"Oh me *too*!" said Mrs. B. "They're just *awful*! Did you squash it?"

"Got away." I surreptitiously took a treat from my pocket and handed it to Plant to calm him back down. Mrs. B expressed her heartfelt wish that the spider would not make its way to *her* side of the room, then moved us all past the incident by asking Ruby to spell dimenhydrinate for me.

I let Ruby do it, mostly to buy myself some time for a heated internal debate. Should I say something? I was only supposed to be taking notes. I wasn't here to interfere.

What a ridiculous excuse. Of course I should say something.

Should I, though? It didn't necessarily mean anything. What could it even mean? Nobody went around poisoning people with Dramamine.

Maybe Clifford took it sometimes, just like his son did. Maybe he'd taken Simone on the ferris wheel after lunch. And did I really want to remind Mrs. B of who he'd had lunch with? I might just be stirring up trouble for no reason.

Well, no—the reason was a murder investigation. Which I had to admit was a pretty good reason. If anything was the kind of thing you stirred up trouble for, this was that kind of thing.

Okay, then.

But I don't want to get Percy in trouble.

In the end, I debated myself right out of the chance. Mrs. B and Ruby, being unaware of my dilemma, went on talking, and the moment to speak passed. It would look weird if I interrupted them with a delayed response, wouldn't it? Definitely weird. Especially after the spider thing. It might even look a little guilty.

"So you're saying Clifford took Dramamine the day he fell?" Mrs. B asked. "How odd! Isn't that *odd*? Clifford didn't get *motion sickness*. He despised weakness. He never got nauseas a day in his life. But that's not a very *illicit* drug, is it? I'm surprised a toxicology screen even looks for something like that."

"It doesn't," said Ruby. "Not specifically, but they screen for antihistamines, and apparently dimenhydrinate is related. I don't really know all the chemistry involved, to be honest. But the point is, he took it. And once they found it in his system, they checked the contents of the flask Minerva found."

"What flask?" Mrs. B's head whipped around to look at me.

"I ..." I felt my face heating, which wasn't going to make me look any less guilty. Of course I hadn't told Mrs. B about the flask. I hadn't told anybody, other than Snick, and Ruby herself. Like I said, as far as I was concerned, everybody else *(not Percy, though, it can't have been Percy)* was a suspect.

Ruby distracted Mrs. B by opening her soft briefcase and pulling out a clear evidence bag containing the flask in question. She handed it to Mrs. B. "Your son confirmed this was your husband's flask."

"Which son?" I blurted.

Ruby glanced at me. "Percy. He didn't tell you?"

No, he didn't. I supposed Ruby had told *him* that I

was the one who found it, same as she'd just told Mrs. B, assuming they already knew.

So he knew about it, and he knew I knew about it, but he didn't say a word. Even when he was delving into the deepest darkest parts of my past, which was a pretty personal conversation, he still didn't say a word.

What did that mean? Did it mean anything?

"No one seems to be telling *anyone anything*!" said Mrs. B. I heartily concurred. "You say Minerva found this, found it where?"

She'd directed the question at Ruby, but I answered for myself. "In the water. Downstream, below the waterfall."

"But what were you doing *there*?" Mrs. B asked.

"I was walking Plant, and ..." I swallowed. "Paying my respects. Saying goodbye."

Mrs. B pressed a hand to her chest. "That's so sweet! Isn't she *sweet*?"

That settled it. I was definitely a terrible person.

"Minerva." Mrs. B pointed at my laptop. "Check the notes. She said the test results could have been compromised, didn't she?"

"Yes," I said slowly. "But—"

She turned back to Ruby. "So you can't be entirely *sure* he had dime-whatever in his system, can you?"

"We're pretty sure," Ruby said. "And the flask was sealed. It was definitely in there, a healthy dose of it, mixed with bourbon. If Clifford had taken the drug himself, he probably would have just swallowed a pill." She sighed. "But even so, I have to rule out the possibility. You're certain you've never known him to take it?"

Mrs. B silently shook her head.

"Well then." Ruby spread her hands. "We have to look at the likelihood that somebody put it in that flask for him. Trying to dose him."

Mrs. B shook her head again. "I don't ... who would want to make sure Clifford didn't get *sick*? And then be so *secretive* about it?"

"They didn't want to make sure he didn't get sick," I said, looking at Ruby. "They wanted to make sure he *did* get good and tired."

Ruby gave me a grave nod. "Like I said, it was a healthy dose. Dimenhydrinate causes drowsiness. Sluggishness."

"I still don't—" Mrs. B looked back at me, her face pale.

I could barely look her in the eye. Especially knowing what I knew about who kept Dramamine in the house. But I forced myself to do it anyway. "He wasn't a small guy, and he was healthy. If somebody had pushed him, there probably would have been signs of a struggle at the edge where he fell. Unless ..."

I drifted off, hoping Mrs. B would complete the thought herself without me having to say it.

But Ruby felt no such compunction, and put it baldly. "Unless whoever pushed him made sure he was out of it first. So out of it that he wouldn't see it coming, or would at least react slowly enough for it not to matter."

My stomach was sinking by the second. But even in my rattled state I had to give mental credit: it was actually a really smart plan. A household drug that anybody could get, that anybody might have. If you were smaller than he was, and weaker, it would put you on equal footing. And if you were neither of those things, it was still a handy way of slowing his reflexes, just like Ruby said, and leaving little to no evidence behind.

The killer probably didn't even realize it would show up on a tox screen. And that was assuming there even was a tox screen. It might never get that far. Not if Clifford never fought back, if he went over easily without digging in his heels, or scratching his assailant and getting skin under his fingernails, or whatever else they were always finding on those procedural TV shows.

"You think ..." Mrs. B squared her shoulders, and sat up very straight. "You think he was murdered."

"I think he may have been," Ruby said gently. Her eyes met mine. "By someone who had access to that flask, and knew Clifford well enough to know he would use it."

I LEFT Plant to comfort Mrs. B as best he could, and walked Ruby out to her car. She must have sensed I had something to tell her, because she didn't argue that she could show herself out.

Every step brought a fresh wave of dread. Was I really going to tell her? I certainly didn't want to.

But what was I supposed to do? A man had died. A man had been *killed*.

I didn't owe Percy anything. When it came down to it, I barely even knew him. My loyalty had to be to truth, and justice, and all that kind of thing. And, I supposed, to my deceased employer, even if he was a ratbag.

What had I been thinking? Why had I even hesitated? *Because he didn't do it. Not Percy.*

And why was I so sure of *that*? Just because he had dimples, and nice hands, and his eyes crinkled when he smiled at me? That was no kind of reason. A crinkle was not a measure of character.

And speaking of character, I was a terrible judge of it. I'd trusted Natalie Jones just fine.

Thought she was a nice lady, in fact. If you'd asked me whether she were capable of putting two bullets in a person's chest, I'd have laughed and said no way. Right up until the second she did it.

No, it was definitely not my place to decide who was or was not guilty. It was not my place to interpret the truth.

Only to tell it.

"So my dog, Plant?" I stopped at the end of Ruby's car, started to lean against it, thought better of that, and stood up straight again. "He likes to grab things. Especially cloth things. Napkins, socks. He kind of prances around with whatever it is, and you're expected to tell him how nice it is. It's a whole thing."

Ruby took her glasses off. "Are you reporting this as a crime? Has Plant absconded with a particularly valuable sock?"

"No, but he pulled one of Percy's out of the trash. A sock, I mean. That he—Percy—had thrown away."

"And Percy wants it back?"

"No, I told you, he threw it in the trash. Why would

he want it?" I shook my head. This wasn't going right. Conversations rarely did, when I was this nervous. "The sock doesn't matter."

Ruby put her glasses back on. "I'm going to be optimistic and assume there's a point in here somewhere, but I suggest you find it fairly soon."

"The trash. The trash is the point."

"And what trash was this?"

"Er … in Percy's bedroom. Or his bathroom, actually. Not that I was in his room for questionable reasons! I was getting some Tagamet for Mrs. B, and he was … Plant just ran into his room. Plant loves Percy."

He did love him. And unlike me, Plant was a pretty good judge of character. This was nitwitted. I was being a nitwit. You could buy Dramamine at any drugstore. It was everywhere.

Too bad, because it was too late. "And?" Ruby asked.

"And Plant knocked the trash over, in his excitement over the sock. And I helped clean it up. And there was a Dramamine box in there. I don't know whether it was empty or not, I didn't look inside. I remember it was kind of crushed, though, and the plastic crinkled when I picked it up, so at least some were gone."

"Chewable?" Ruby asked, her voice taking on a clipped, professional tone that I did not like.

"Um. I don't know. Does it matter?"

She didn't answer. "When was this?"

I thought back, mentally calculating. "Last Monday, I think? It was definitely in between when you found Clifford's body and the funeral."

"Had Percy been traveling recently?"

"Not that I'm aware of. But there were a lot of drugs in his trash!" Judging by Ruby's face, that hadn't come out any closer to right than anything else I'd said in the last three minutes. "I mean, he said he was cleaning out his medicine cabinet. So the Dramamine could have been really old, for all I know. Anyway he said he uses it for the ferris wheel. The ferris wheel at Tybryd, you know?"

"Yes, I'm aware of the ferris wheel. It's on every postcard."

"Well, I'm sure he rides it a lot. I'm sure a lot of people in town do. Probably half of them have Dramamine lying around." I nodded extra vigorously, for emphasis. "More than half, even, with these mountain roads and all. Those switchbacks are brutal."

I was right, of course. That box in Percy's trash didn't prove anything.

Neither did the fight he'd had with Clifford, the night I arrived at Baird House.

And neither did a search history that pointed at Clifford wanting to disinherit one of his children.

Or a disposable phone that pointed at Clifford questioning whether one of his children was his at all.

But I had to admit that when you put it all together, it didn't look exactly great.

Chapter Twelve

PLANT LOOKED VERY dapper in his bowtie. And that's about as high as the highlights of the ball got.

He was to line up in the receiving line in the front entry with Sweetie, Saltie, Tart, and Bitts, each of whom was sporting a scarlet cape. Mrs. B thought the dogs would be a cute treat for the guests. And who knows, maybe some of the guests saw it that way, too.

I myself qualified as neither cute, nor a treat. I was pretty sure I did qualify, in some sort of official sense, as a catastrophe. Maybe even a tragedy. The Bairds might have been eligible for federal emergency aid, based on my —and my outfit's—presence in their home.

A fact I was painfully conscious of as I descended the stairs to meet the family in all their glory. The ball had made the switch from masquerade masks to costumes back in the sixties, and true to their Arthurian names, each year this generation of Bairds dressed as knights and lords and ladies.

Percy looked especially dashing, which was not going

to help matters. I'd been nervous around him since my conversation with Ruby, which tended to result in a lot of clumsiness and the sort of remarks you lie awake and castigate yourself for later. And of course he had no idea why, given that I'd rather have plucked out my own eyeballs than tell him (or anybody, for that matter) that I'd ratted him out. Maybe he thought I was still mad about the whole Natalie thing. Or maybe he thought I was an eighth-grader with a crush.

"Minerva!" Paisley looked like Guinevere Barbie. Also not helping. "*Adorable* costume. What ... who are you supposed to be?"

I cleared my throat. "Nobody."

Snick and I were there as staff, not guests, which meant our dress code called for formalwear rather than costumes. The trouble with that was, I hadn't had the time to get a new formal dress, even if I could've afforded one, which I could not. The only thing I had that fit—and I use that term loosely—was a bridesmaid's dress from the previous spring.

Look, I know most bridesmaid's dresses are at least a little bad, but when I say this one was bad, I don't mean mildly embarrassing. Or even severely embarrassing. I'm talking about a full-blown calamity of lime green taffeta with black buttons down the front, and a very small wine stain that I was sure nobody would notice, what with all the shiny black flowers embroidered all over the bodice to distract them from it. Apparently I'd worn it with very high heels, because it was a couple inches too long, making it hazardous as well as grotesque.

At least my hair looked good. We must find our comfort where we can.

"Well, I think she's adorable!" Mrs. B declared. "Doesn't she look just *adorable*?"

Percy and Tristan both murmured their assent, not that I could meet either of their eyes.

"Of course she is!" Paisley said, in the fakest tone I'd ever heard another human use. "Did you make that dress yourself?"

You would think that would've been the lowlight of the evening, but you would be wrong. It wasn't even close.

The guest list was a hodge-podge of gazillionaires, captains of industry, and locals, with two Hollywood producers and one famous director thrown in for good measure. Oh, and Paisley's parents. Who were exactly what you would expect. And who I noted showed up for the fun event but not the funeral.

While they all flowed in, I supervised the dogs from the shadow of the grand staircase, willing Plant to behave like a gentleman and not show anybody their own socks. (He did great, another highlight.) When the receiving line broke up at last, I took all five dogs upstairs to my room, envying them the nice bed, if not the stuffed bones I gave them.

Actually, I might even have taken a bone, if it meant I could swap that stupid dress for some pajamas and curl up with a pile of taffy and a nice book. Behind a door, where Paisley Grant could not see me, and I could not see her smug smile while she silently (but very very obviously) laughed at me.

But of course there would be none of that. Snick and I were buried. We had to keep things running on schedule. We had to supervise the temporary staff. We had to soothe Keith Howell's deep indignation over one of the movie producers also being dressed as a Tudor king, and get Paisley a "better" chocolate cosmopolitan than the one she'd been given.

There was much more to do than hands to do it, and *That's not my job* was a phrase not to be uttered. On the bright side, running around like a scattered bug made the night go by faster.

On the less bright side, as a consequence of the general chaos of the evening, I happened to be the one in the front hall when, long after the receiving line or any sort of formal greeting was available, Ruby Walker came to call.

Asking to see Percy.

I tried to tell myself that it wasn't necessarily for any bad reason. Ruby didn't seem like the type to enjoy the drama of confronting a man about Dramamine in front of his mom and a ballroom full of guests. I asked whether it could wait.

Ruby said it could not.

She looked even more aloof than usual, and her tone was all business. My heart sank about as fast as my hands started to shake. Maybe she wouldn't enjoy the drama, but if she considered it her job, I supposed she wouldn't shy away from it, either.

The timing could not have been worse. Mrs. B and her three children were standing in front of the orchestra on the little stage, microphones and champagne in hand.

They appeared to be toasting the late Clifford Baird. At least, I thought that was Mrs. B's point. It was hard to say for sure, because her voice was thick with tears.

Every eye was on them. The room was silent but for her.

I stood at the edge of the floor, wringing my hands, wondering if I could hold Ruby off until the music started back up and people started dancing again. Surely that would be best for everybody. Ruby would see that.

Well, maybe she would have and maybe she wouldn't. I never got to find out.

Whether Ruby made some movement behind me, or it was just some instinct of his, I couldn't have said. But Percy looked our way—and caught my eye. Or, I guessed, my whole face. I had no doubt I looked a state.

Without a second's hesitation, he handed his microphone to the cellist and his champagne to the violinist, and leapt off the platform. Once again, the proverbial knight charging in to rescue the lady in distress. He was even dressed for it this time.

Except I wasn't the one who needed rescuing. And I didn't feel like much of a lady. I didn't even feel like much of a human. Ruby cuffed him—*Cuffed him!*—and everything.

Lowlight: watching Ruby arrest Percy Baird for the murder of his father, for all his loved ones, his enemies, and the heavens to see.

Based on information I had given her.

Chapter Thirteen

THE GUESTS SEEMED to view Percy's arrest as part of the entertainment, and to fully intend to go right on eating the Bairds' food and drinking the Bairds' booze while they gossiped about the Bairds' troubles. It was left to me and Snick to move them along, while Elaine (who'd lost Phil early in the evening to a rock-swallowing dog) and Tristan calmed their hysterical mother.

I was pretty sure I was about to break the record for the fastest ulcer ever grown. Despite the chaos around me, I couldn't keep everything to myself. The first chance I got, I grabbed Snick by the elbow and dragged him into the pantry to confess my sins. He knew some of them already, but the whole Dramamine thing was new to him.

"Well, you certainly are in a pickle, aren't you?" Snick, true to his character, looked more amused than horrified.

"Me?" I swatted him. "What about Percy? Did you

see his face? I can't imagine what he's thinking right now."

He'd looked so lost. Not even angry. Just lost. I clenched a fistful of my awful taffeta skirt. If I was going to be thrown out onto the street, which I considered a strong possibility, I hoped I would at least be allowed to change first. "I have to tell Mrs. B this is all my fault."

"Sure you do," said Snick. "She'll find out eventually anyway. Like when you testify against Percy in court."

I swatted him harder. "You're not helping!"

"Why would you think I was trying to help?" He caught my expression and turned down the snark, if only slightly. "But do you have to tell her right this second? It's not a great time for her to lose her assistant."

He had an excellent point there. So while he finished dealing with the remnants of the ball, I called the family lawyer (who hadn't been at the ball, but assured me he was going straight to the police station), followed his instructions to prepare for whatever bail might be set, tried with no success whatsoever to get rid of Paisley, and drove a shaking, weeping Mrs. B to the police station.

At least that last task came after everybody changed out of their costumes. If nothing else, I would have the dignity of pants for the ordeal to come.

Elaine and Tristan chose to stay home. Mostly because they didn't see what good having a bunch of extra people hanging around the police station was going to do, and a little bit because they were both drunk. I considered it a wise decision on both counts.

I only wished I'd been able to convince that blasted barnacle Paisley of the same. But she seemed bent on making the whole thing about her, and acting like a grieving wife whose husband was about to be unjustly executed. Never mind that we expected Percy to sleep in his own bed that night—or that he couldn't stand her.

She rode into Bryd Hollow in my back seat, which was one reason (the other being cowardice) I still held off on saying anything to Mrs. B, despite the latter's steady wailing about who could *possibly* think *Percy* was capable of *murder*. Percy was a wonderful person! He'd never been violent! He was incapable of hurting anybody!

I decided to just focus on getting the poor woman (and Percy's creepy stalker) there, and getting things rolling as best I could. Once I handed Mrs. B off to the lawyer, I could tell her then, and let the chips fall where they may. He'd be able to take care of her if I found myself banished.

But that handoff seemed to belong to some distant future as I sat on an uncomfortably hard bench between Mrs. B and Paisley, wondering why booking Percy was taking so long. We'd assumed the whole thing would be fairly quick. A magistrate was required, to set the initial bond, but there'd been two of them at the ball. It wasn't like anybody needed to be pulled out of bed.

One of them did show up, but not until a couple of hours after we did. Apparently he considered it in poor taste to fulfill official criminal justice duties in his Al Capone costume, and had gone home to shower and change first. When he, like the lawyer before him, disappeared through the door to whatever dungeon they were keeping Percy in, I finally accepted that anything a lowly assistant could do in this situation had been done.

I got up to get Mrs. B a cup of bad coffee and steel my nerves.

"Mrs. B," I said as I handed her the coffee, "I'm sorry, the last thing I want to do is upset you more, but I have to tell you something. Things. I have to tell you some things."

She looked at me with glazed eyes. "What sort of things?"

I cleared my throat. "Just ... things I haven't told you about yet. About Clifford. And a little bit about Percy."

"Like that flask you gave to Ruby?"

"Sort of, yeah." I reminded her of Clifford's search history, which she already knew about. Then I told her about the disposable phone and JoraLab. (I didn't know what that whole business had to do with Percy's arrest—there was no way Percy wasn't really Clifford's son—but I figured if I was going to come clean, I might as well do it all the way.) I finished with the Great Dramamine Debacle.

I tried to downplay that Ruby had gotten every single one of those things from me. That the whole case against Percy was my doing. But I was pretty sure she read between the lines.

Especially after Paisley sprang off the bench, planted her manicured hands on my shoulders, and gave me a hard shove.

"You mean to tell me this is *your* fault?" she screeched (setting aside the fact that I clearly hadn't meant to tell *her* anything at all). She went on from there, but a lot of the words she used are not repeatable in respectable company. Finally an officer came and told her they'd already had enough excitement for one evening, and if she couldn't calm herself down, she would have to leave.

When she got out of my face, I saw that Mrs. B had left the bench. I turned around to find her standing a few feet away, talking to the lawyer.

Paisley saw him too, and grabbed my arm as she stared at them. As if we were in this together. As if we were friends, and she hadn't been throwing a tantrum in my direction mere seconds ago. I let it pass in favor of keeping quiet so we could eavesdrop.

Percy's bail had been set. He'd be going home soon.

Odsbodikins. I was the one who'd driven us here from Baird House. This was going to be one awkward drive home.

Or not.

As she'd once lamented to me herself, people tended to underestimate Bessie Baird. Apparently that included me, because I hadn't thought of her as much of a mama bear. She hadn't seemed prepared to do much to protect her kids from their father.

But she was prepared to protect them from me.

As soon as the lawyer went back through that mysterious door to the dungeon, she turned to me. With flint in her eye. "Minerva, it'll be a bit yet, before everything is settled. We can find another way back. You should take this opportunity to go and gather your things. It will be best if you're not there when Percy gets home."

No italics, no exclamation points. It seemed I was no longer adorable.

If Percy had been there (you know, if I hadn't gotten him arrested), maybe he would have told his mother that firing me for telling the truth was shaky ground. Maybe I could have sued or something.

But I didn't argue with her. For the moment, we had intersecting goals.

I wanted nothing more than to be gone before I had to look Percy Baird in the eye.

Chapter Fourteen

I only lived in one room at Baird House, and that was furnished; I didn't have much to pack. Anything I couldn't fit in my car, Snick could forward to me at … wherever. Somewhere.

Plant and I left that night without encountering Percy, or any other Baird. Mrs. B could explain to Elaine and Tristan—and Tristan's dogs—why we were gone.

The only one I said goodbye to was Snick. To the surprise of nobody, he laughed. But he gave me a hug, too, and told me not to feel bad.

A ridiculous request. Of course I was going to feel bad. For Percy. For myself. And for Plant, who did not appreciate being dragged out of bed in the middle of the night, only to hear we were homeless now.

The homeless part didn't last long. I only stayed with Paul and Carrie for three days, before good fortune and Paul both intervened on my behalf, and got me a job at Noah's Bark. The pay wasn't enough to live on, making it unsuitable as a longterm solution. But it was something I could bring Plant to while I figured out what in all blazes I was going to do next.

Best of all, Gretchen didn't just own the pet shop, she owned the two-room apartment above it. And she was willing to rent it to me cheap, as long as I was willing to go downstairs to open and close the store every day. I wasn't even out of Baird House a week before Plant and I had settled into our temporary, but at least temporarily stable, situation.

The first thing I did on my first day off ("off" meaning all I had to do was open, then come back at seven to close) was call Snick to demand he let me take him to lunch. He agreed not only immediately but enthusiastically, which I took as a sign he had gossip to share.

Good. I needed to get started.

Bryd Hollow was home now, and running away from home (again) was out of the question. If I'd accidentally scribbled all over my clean slate, well, I'd just have to find a way to wipe it off again. Percy Baird was soon to be tried for murder because of me. I meant to rectify that.

I didn't give any serious consideration to the possibility that Percy was actually guilty. That ship, which was pretty shoddily constructed to begin with, had sunk almost the second I uttered the word "Dramamine" to Ruby. It didn't matter that I didn't know him well, or that my abysmal character-judging skills were well established. It also didn't matter that he had motive, means, and opportunity. I simply could not, at my core, believe it of him.

The obvious way to clear his name was to find the

guilty party, but I very much doubted Ruby was going to recruit me onto the police force any time soon. Being an unofficial nobody with no authority whatsoever closed off a great many avenues of investigation. Most avenues of investigation, really—except the one Ruby refused to care about. Which also happened to be the one I was most qualified to pursue.

I'd brainstormed a multitude of reasons that a person with a flair for the dramatic might want to kill Clifford Baird in the same way Alistair had died. These ranged from the weird-but-plausible (the killer was crazy, and just thought it was funny) to the weird-and-preposterous (there was no killer; a witch had put a curse on the Baird men, and both really had slipped).

But the one that made the most sense to me was that Clifford and his great-grandfather had committed the same transgression. Something that would make a parallel death feel like poetic justice.

And while it was possible that Alistair had genuinely had an accident, it seemed likeliest that the parallel was complete, and both Bairds had been murdered for ... whatever they'd done.

Which was what? Back when I first found Clifford's personal JoraLab hotline, Snick and I had talked about both men's penchant for adultery, and even the possibility that Clifford's mistress was pregnant. But if that were the case, surely she would have come forward by now, paternity test in hand. There were too many questions, too many things that didn't quite fit. There had to be more to the story.

Then again, maybe the kind of ratbag who would

repeatedly cheat on his wife was the kind of ratbag who would do any number of other rotten things, too. Maybe their deaths had nothing to do with their womanizing at all.

There was a lot of conjecture rolling around in my head, but it all boiled down to one thing: if I could solve the mystery of Alistair's death, I might be able to solve the mystery of Clifford's, too.

I just needed a few things from Snick first. I told him to meet me at the pet shop, and brought Plant down early, to hang out at the store while I was gone.

For a few minutes, Gretchen and I were each occupied with greeting the dog who did not belong to her, but Noah, who was gray in the muzzle and well into his lazy years, tired of me first. He went back to his bed in the huge front window, leaving me alone to study Gretchen's wrinkles—all seven million of them. "Gretchen, you've been living in Bryd Hollow a long time, right?"

"All eighty-two of my years." She gave Plant a final scratch and looked up at me, thin brow raised. "Assuming that was why you were asking, as a subtle way of finding out my age."

"Of course not," I said. I *had* been thinking about how old she was, but that wasn't quite the same thing. "It was more that I was curious about the perspective of an old-timer. What do you think about Clifford Baird falling over Adley Falls?"

"Well, he wouldn't be the first one, would he?" She put her hands on her hips. "I don't for a second believe Percy did it, and don't think I didn't hear that you had a hand in getting him arrested for it."

I thought no such thing; I knew perfectly well that word had spread around town with shocking speed. I got enough dirty looks because of it. Even from the people who thought Percy *was* guilty. It didn't matter to them whether or not he'd killed his father—either way, they didn't want him to go to jail for it. They liked Percy, and they'd hated Clifford, and that seemed to be all that mattered to Bryd Hollow's general concept of justice.

Meanwhile, everybody seemed to have a smile for Plant when we walked down the street. Which struck me as monumentally unfair, considering it was Plant who'd found the Dramamine and led me to the flask. But it seemed petty to stop people and insist that if they were going to be mad at me, they had to be mad at my dog, too.

"I don't think he did it, either," I said.

Gretchen patted my shoulder as she walked past to straighten a display of pet costumes for Halloween. "You've got a funny way of showing it, dear."

I took the teasing in stride. I was glad she had faith in Percy; it made me feel less foolish for my own. But for the moment, I was more interested in the fact that she seemed to know about the other lives Adley Falls had claimed. "Did you know that Alistair Baird was one of the people who died up there?"

"I remembered, after I found out that was where Clifford took the plunge. My father used to tell me stories about the place being haunted."

"Ruby said the exact same thing. Plant, stop." Plant, bored and annoyed that I'd taken Gretchen's attention off him, had taken to nibbling at the toe of my boot. I shooed him away, and he flopped down next to Noah in the window. "Weird, though. Not one of the Bairds themselves seemed to realize."

Gretchen shrugged. "Oh, they probably did. They probably just didn't mention it to you. Why would they? No offense, I'm sure you didn't mean to cause all the trouble you did, but you do seem to have a tendency to stick your nose in and make a big thing out of a little one."

The bell over the door tinkled, and she smiled at somebody behind me. "Well, if it isn't the butler. Aren't *you* supposed to be the one who did it?"

Thus freed from defending myself from the charges of Troublemaker and Busybody, I grabbed my purse, while Snick gave Gretchen air kisses on either side of her face and assured her that Percy and the rest of the Bairds were holding up just fine.

I wondered if that was true. I guessed I'd find out soon enough.

"Pizzabilities, or the diner?" I asked as we walked outside.

"What, no Rapunzel's?"

"I couldn't afford Rapunzel's, even if I were dressed for it. Do they even do lunch?"

"I think so. The Sunday brunch is divine. Deirdre's, then, it's closer."

It was, in fact, directly across the street. In my one week as a citizen of Bryd Hollow proper, I'd learned two key things about Deirdre's. First, that Deirdre was many years in her grave, and that the diner's owner was her grandson, a burly, hairy man named Tony whose loyalty to his Baird overlords was surpassed only by his intense disapproval of what he called "bird eaters." Apparently that meant people who ate *like* birds, rather than people who ate poultry and such.

He mistook me for just such a person (I'd been a few pounds underweight since the Natalie Jones affair), until I discovered the second key thing, which was Tony's pimento cheese fries. They made every disapproving look he cared to give me worthwhile.

Snick and I grabbed a couple of menus on our way in, and settled into a booth we were lucky to get. As I understood it, tourism always slowed down between the summer and the foliage, but things were picking up again now that October had arrived. The place was packed with people seeking to fortify themselves with burgers and fried chicken before they went to tour Tybryd.

Fools. It was all about the fries. When Tony came at me with a *What'll you have, twig?* I got a double order, and nothing else. I saw no point in complicating things with a sandwich.

Tony was a lot nicer to Snick. At first I assumed it was just because the latter hadn't gotten the town's golden boy arrested lately, but Tony's ulterior motive for waiting on us personally quickly became clear: he wanted gossip. While Snick ordered a superfood salad and went through the same assurances of the Bairds' wellbeing that he'd given Gretchen, I put a couple of quarters into the tabletop jukebox, in hopes that it would keep anybody from listening in on our conversation.

As soon as Tony left, Snick leaned forward, eyes

alight. "So. The first thing I wanted to tell you is ... are you ready for it?"

"Paisley's gone?" I asked hopefully.

"No. Well, yes, actually. Mrs. B herself told her to go.

"No!"

"Yep. Told her the family needed some privacy right now. Paisley threw exactly the fit you would expect, and it was *spectacular*. But that's not the big thing. The big thing is ..." Snick smacked the table with both hands. "It's not your fault Percy got arrested!"

I blinked at him, mouth agape—clearly the effect he'd been hoping for. A wide, delighted grin broke across his face. When I didn't say anything, he went on, "They found Clifford's phone in Percy's office at Tybryd."

I shook my head, still kind of stuck back at *It's not your fault*. "They? They who?"

"One of the cleaning crew. She called Ruby as soon as she realized whose it was. This was like an hour before Ruby showed up to arrest Percy, which explains why she did it that night, of all nights. I guess she just couldn't wait."

"And they found Percy's fingerprints on it?"

"I heard they didn't find any prints at all, other than the cleaning lady's. And she's already been ruled out as a suspect."

I leaned back and folded my arms. "Then somebody put it there to frame him."

Snick snorted. "Someone's got a crush on Percy."

"This has nothing to do with a crush, Snick, we're talking about an innocent man being tried for murder!" I caught my voice getting louder, and started half-talking, half-hissing instead. "You can't seriously believe he did it! You like Percy!"

"Okay Bessie Baird, maybe tone down the exclamations." Snick curled his lip at the jukebox. "You've got Mrs. B's taste in music, too. You couldn't find anything less than fifty years old?"

"In a town that blares oldies on the street all day long?" I tapped the box. "And this is a *diner jukebox*. Oldies are the whole point."

"Whatever. And yes, I do like Percy, but what has that got to do with anything? Killing Clifford doesn't make a person *unlikable*."

I rolled my eyes. "That seems to be a popular opinion." I waited while Tony set down our plates, then immediately started on my fries, which no amount of confusion was going to put me off from. "Speaking of popular opinion, if the case turns out to be mostly based on the phone, why is everybody still blaming me?"

"Headline on page one, retraction on page thirty-two, as usual," Snick said. "I just heard about all this yesterday, but the ones a little closer to the case obviously must have known for a while."

"So you're telling me neither Percy nor Mrs. B are doing anything to disabuse anybody of the notion that I'm the one who did this to him."

Snick put on a wide-eyed face. "Yeah, it's weird how Percy doesn't seem to get that his whole nightmare is actually about you."

I thought about wadding up my napkin and throwing it at him, but decided against it, considering I'd thoroughly deserved that. "Mrs. B then. Why is she still mad at me?"

"What did you think, she'd throw herself at your feet and beg you to come back to work?"

Well, if he was going to put it like that, I supposed it sounded a little silly. "If I didn't do anything wrong—"

"Are you kidding me? You did *the* thing wrong." Snick shook his finger at me. "*You* talked out of turn. Servants do not do that. It's like the first rule."

I crossed my arms. "Whatever happened to Mrs. B never wanting us to feel like servants?"

"Semantics," he said with a wave. "She still follows the old-school rich-people code, and she expected you to do the same. If it would be inconvenient to them for you to see or hear or notice something, you don't see or hear or notice it."

"You gossip about them all the time!" I protested.

"Of course I do. In the kitchen, where it belongs. I don't gossip to *Ruby*. You *never* go outside the house. They can't have someone living with them that they can't trust to keep their secrets."

"That's ridiculous. It's not 1898." I shook my head. This argument was getting us off track. "But you're right about one thing."

"Just the one?"

"This isn't about me. We need to figure out who's doing this to Percy. I mean, obviously it's the real murderer, but we'd have to give Ruby more than that."

"Listen to you, all"—Snick brought out the finger quotes—"*the real murderer.*" He managed to both laugh and shove a forkful of salad into his mouth at the same time. "You've been reading too many mystery novels. What makes you so positive Percy didn't do it? The simplest explanation is usually the right one, and all that."

I huffed at him. "You can really see Percy killing somebody? His own father?"

Snick shrugged. "If he was going to kill anyone, I'd say his own father was the strongest candidate. Maybe he didn't even do it on purpose. Maybe they had a fight, and it got physical, and Clifford fell by accident."

"What, and then Percy just dove into the water and took the phone off the corpse before it floated away?" I made a wide gesture with the fry in my hand, spraying bits of cheese over the table. "Look at the big picture. The Dramamine. The Dramamine *in* the flask. And doing it at the same spot where Alistair died? This was premeditated and deliberate, and it was hateful."

Snick looked unconvinced. I jabbed the fry at him this time. "And even if you believe that of Percy, you have to admit, he's no nitwit. Why on earth would he go through all the trouble of wiping the prints off Clifford's phone, and then just leave it in his desk for the cleaning person to find?"

His face suggested I actually had a point there. "Okay, but if that's crossed your mind, I think we can assume it's crossed Ruby's. Or at least one of the seventeen lawyers who are always at the house now. You don't need to solve the case, you know."

I chewed at my lip. "Maybe I do. Clifford's phone might be Percy's coffin, but everything I told Ruby was one more nail in it. This is still partly my fault. And besides, nobody else is considering Alistair at all." I told him about my thoughts on that matter.

"So it's actually Alistair's death you want to investigate."

"Like I said, nobody else is doing it. And that's why I called you."

Snick's brows shot up. "You're thinking I want to play Watson?"

I ignored the stupid, pointless pang I felt at him bringing up Sherlock Holmes—as most people making detective analogies would. Most people, but not Percy. "No, but I am thinking you can get me Emily's journals back."

In a fit of conscience, I'd left them behind when I left the house. Then almost immediately regretted it. It seemed unlikely that anybody would miss them, and they weren't doing anybody any good gathering dust on a shelf. "And something else, too. I found a guest list from the original ball online."

"How'd you manage that?" Snick asked.

"It took some digging, but not as much as you might think. It was the first one, and the Bairds do love their ball."

"That they do."

"The point is, can you also get me the photograph that was hanging in the hallway, the one with everybody from the 1913 ball in it? You said you take the ball ones down afterward, right, and store them until the next year? So probably nobody would miss that any more than they would Emily's journals. Maybe I can match up some names and faces."

"The faces were partly covered," Snick pointed out. "And what good is that going to do you, anyway?"

"Maybe none." I twisted my straw wrapper around my fingers and amended that to, "*Probably* none. But I've got to start somewhere. Alistair died like a year and a half later. I'm just trying to get a sense of who the players were, you know? Who was in his life, who his enemies might have been. That picture would have his whole crowd in it."

Snick leaned back and drummed his fingers against the table. "But you agree that I'm not your Watson. Because being Watson could get me fired."

"Not my Watson," I assured him. "Plant can be my Watson." *Or my Hastings.*

"So if I do this for you, you won't come back a week later asking for anything else?"

"Well I can't promise *that*."

"At least you're honest, I guess." Snick sighed. "Okay, give me a couple of days. I'll drop them off at the Bark."

"Perfect." I rubbed my hands together, and tossed his Holmes reference right back at him. "The game is afoot."

Chapter Fifteen

Have I mentioned what a truly, truly horrible artist Mrs. Emily Baird was? I mean abysmal. And I say this as somebody whose greatest accomplishments in the visual arts feature stick figures.

One of the journals was almost entirely sketches, with only the occasional mention of some trivial detail or other. I thought maybe I could use that to place it chronologically, except I didn't know whether she'd shifted more toward sketching over time, or less.

I didn't know much of anything at all, really.

It wasn't for lack of trying. I pored over those three weathered volumes, night after night as I sat on the bed in my two-room haven above Noah's Bark, Plant snoring at (or more often, on) my feet after a long day of entertaining customers. The dreary, wet September had turned into a lovely October, and the hissing, occasionally spitting radiator kept me cozy through the cool nights. I found the noise oddly comforting.

When I got hungry, there was the low counter at the

other end of the room that qualified that side as the kitchen, with a dorm-sized fridge below and a microwave, toaster oven, and electric kettle on top. (My options when it came to serving were washing dishes in the bathroom sink, or eating straight off the toaster oven rack with my fingers.) I was well-stocked on tea and taffy. It was a far cry from Rebecca's cooking, but I was content.

And when I wanted a splurge, Deirdre's was just across Honor Avenue. Maybe the news that Percy's arrest wasn't entirely—or even mostly—my doing had finally gotten around, because Tony seemed to be warming up to me. He still called me Twig, but it was different now. You could hear him capitalizing it as a proper noun, a nickname rather than a namecalling name. He even let me bring Plant *just* inside the door, if I was getting takeout.

Which was more often than was fiscally responsible of me; it was hard to resist stopping by when I was out in the evening, and I was out a lot of evenings. Whenever I needed a break from Emily's journals, I walked Plant in a loop around Bryd Hollow, to Purity Street and then Modesty Avenue, up Amity and back to Honor again, trying to put myself inside Emily's head.

A lot had changed since the town was founded in 1897—I could only assume the streets didn't echo with the voices of the Andrews Sisters and the Coasters back then—but the same bones were there. The streets her husband named, the beautiful church he built, the old brick and the even older trees. I tried to see it all as she would have seen it, to imagine her thoughts as she strolled around. Her real thoughts, not the ones she'd encoded in bad drawings.

At night, I would dream about her. Sometimes she was smacking me with a wooden spoon, and telling me off for talking out of turn as a servant never, ever should. Sometimes she was just smiling that small, secret smile.

What do you know, Emily, that I don't?

From an opportunity perspective, I considered her and their son George, aged twenty-six at the time of his father's death, to be strong suspects in Alistair's murder. The Bairds often entertained visitors at Tybryd, but among their glittering social circle, houses were seasonal things. Alistair had met his end and his maker in February of 1915. At that time of year, his family were the only peers he'd have been taking walks with.

Them, and maybe whatever mistress or mistresses he'd had at the time. Given the secrecy that surrounded his infidelities, their identities were as much of a mystery as his wife's journals. Or his wife, period.

I didn't see Percy, or any of the Bairds. I never went near either Baird House or Tybryd. I did hear news and rumors, though, from Snick and Gretchen and sometimes just random people in the pet shop. Percy had been arraigned and was still out on bail, living at home, but it seemed his case was being expedited in some way, because the trial was slated to begin just after Thanksgiving.

Unless I could stop it. Time felt like it was speeding up, and if solving the carriwitchet that was Emily Baird was to be anything more than an academic exercise, I needed to speed up right along with it.

My first real breakthrough came when I managed to

match another person to her floral counterpart: George's wife was associated with lilies. Which might not have meant much on its own, but paired with what I already knew about the cornflowers, was a pretty big deal. Laying the journals out on my bed like tarot cards one cold Tuesday night, I used Alistair's mother's death and George's wedding to construct a timeline for the cornflowers and the lilies—and thereby put the books into what I was pretty sure was the correct chronological order.

The one that was mostly sketches was from later in Emily's life, when George was the master of Tybryd and Emily the mother-in-law shunted off to Baird House. If that was the third volume, the 1913 ball would have taken place somewhere during the second.

Possibly around the time Emily mentioned—repeatedly—how much she detested roses, and how she meant to have them all removed from her gardens. I was pretty sure this was also the volume with the entry that had struck me the first time I read the journals: *I cut the roses today.*

Wasn't there a Rose on the guest list?

"Plant, where is that printout of the guest list?"

Plant didn't even raise his head. Just rolled his eyes up toward me, just enough to make it clear that he did not care about the guest list, and I was on my own. Fine, it was a small room. I found it without his help.

There she was. Rose Eastridge. Might she be the Rose Emily despised so much?

Given what I knew about both her husband's infidelity and her reaction to it, it seemed reasonable to assume that the only woman Emily would have become that fixated on was one of Alistair's mistresses. Especially if the woman had the gall to show up at Emily's party.

I grabbed a fresh pile of taffy, practically crackling with excitement over a whole night of glorious historical research ahead of me. (No, that is not sarcasm.) But my laptop battery turned out to be almost dead, and there was no good place to sit near the only free outlet. I considered my phone screen too small for the intense searching required to turn up information—preferably alongside a photograph—about a random early-twentieth-century woman to whom I bore no relation.

Which meant I had no choice but to wait a little bit to see if I could find this Rose. Clearly, there was nothing to be done but run across the street and grab a double order of fries to go. The wind was rattling the windows in their frames, and I'd recently discovered that my "winter" coat was insufficient even for a mountain October, but nevertheless. I'd just have to be brave.

As usual, Plant did not approve of bravery in the face of weather. I asked him if he wanted to go for a walk, and was solidly declined. It seemed he preferred to wait for me to get up, then roll into my spot on the bed.

Sadly, my love of fries was to be denied. As I walked past the diner windows, I saw Elaine Baird and her veterinarian boyfriend sitting in a booth. They were holding hands across the table, and he was laughing at something she'd just said. Which struck me, because Elaine wasn't generally funny. She looked like a different person from the one I'd met before Clifford died. She seemed so much *lighter*. More like her mother—and her brother.

I'm not saying I'd blossomed into a fizzing detective or anything, but my sleuthing instinct told me that running into Elaine was likely to be awkward. I kept walking. Pizzabilities was just at the corner of Honor and Purity, and a thin crust with sausage and onions was almost as good as fries.

Maybe even better. It smelled heavenly inside, in that way that pizza parlors always do. Ruby Walker came in while I was waiting for my pie, and I watched (a little resentfully) while several people gave her a warm greeting.

"How come they're not mad at you?" I asked, when she finished ordering and came to stand in the waiting area.

Ruby's brow furrowed a little. "Who?"

I gestured widely, reminding myself of Percy. "Everybody. They're all mad at me, or at least they were, and Gretchen says it's because everybody loves Percy. But you're the one who arrested him, and nobody seems mad at you."

"Maybe everybody loves me more than they love Percy." She must have read the skepticism in my face, because she laughed. I admired her perfect teeth, and realized I wasn't sure if I'd seen them before. Or heard Ruby laugh before. Maybe she was more relaxed when she was anticipating pizza. "They know I'm just doing my job. Whereas you, to be blunt, are an outsider who came into town and started sticking her nose into other people's business."

I huffed. "That isn't fair. What was I supposed to do, keep things from you? Impede an active investigation?"

"Of course not." She shrugged. "But you asked. I answered."

The teen behind the counter called my name and handed me my pizza, the box warm and dimpled with little grease spots at the bottom. Resisting the urge to open it and stick my face right inside, I turned to go.

Then I stopped and turned back around. If Ruby was in such a giving mood, maybe she'd give me an unguarded answer to one more question. "You don't really think Percy did it, do you?"

No luck. She just rolled her eyes and said, "I can't discuss the case. As I'm sure you're aware."

Fine. I guessed I'd just have to embarrass her by proving her wrong in front of everybody.

When I got back to my apartment, I found my laptop charged enough to serve its purpose. Thankfully, the recent blow to my finances had come after my subscriptions to two history and genealogy sites were renewed, so I had resources at my disposal. I shared my pizza with Plant (crust only for him), and threw myself down a long and winding rabbit hole.

Until I found Rose Eastridge at the bottom of it. It wasn't a unique name, but my Rose—Emily's Rose, and maybe Alistair's too—was the daughter of a pair of wealthy Midwesterners named Jacob and Lucille Eastridge, and the first cousin of an even wealthier New York banker named John Eastridge, all of whom (along with John's wife) were at the 1913 ball. Rose would have been twenty-one at the time. Young. But probably old enough to have an affair with the fifty-two year old Alistair.

In January of 1914, Rose made it into the New York society pages for attending a new year's gala, again with John and his wife. And then: nothing. No marriage record. Not even a death certificate.

I could generally count on there being reliable records about rich people, at least for major events. But it was like Rose Eastridge had just ... ceased to exist.

I cut the roses today.

Did *cut* mean *killed*, in Emilyspeak?

It wasn't Rose's murder I needed to solve, and the two I already had on my plate felt like plenty. Still, it was hard to ignore the possibility. Especially since there might be a connection. If Emily had killed Rose, she'd almost certainly killed Alistair, too.

Maybe even at the same time. Maybe both Alistair and his mistress had gone over the falls that day. If just Alistair's body had washed up, that would account for Rose's disappearance.

I considered it a crime to use sticky notes, or even a bookmark, on books as old as Emily's journals, so I hadn't marked any of the pages. I thumbed through the second volume until I finally found the page that referred to rose-cutting, near the end.

It wasn't phrased exactly the way I remembered it. There was a bit more to go on than I remembered, too.

Cut the roses today. They were set to strangle the rhododendrons if I didn't cut them back. The garden is safe and clear now, and it looks so much better already.

The rhododendrons?

Both Tybryd and Baird House were famous for the deep red rhododendrons that lined their drives, an almost identical shade to both buildings' signature red roofs. What did they represent, in this little metaphor Emily had going on?

Maybe the garden meant Tybryd—maybe the rhododendrons were Emily herself. I grabbed my laptop again and opened a fresh tab in my browser to go to Tybryd's site. I knew they had a section with some background about the grounds and the famous gardens.

Sure enough, the page specifically said that the rhododendrons were there from the start, planted for Mrs. Emily Baird, as they were her favorite flower.

So she'd felt forced to do something (possibly involving gardening shears) to save herself from strangulation, literal or figurative, at Rose's hands. It was a simple matter of self-preservation. Or at least, that was the story she'd told herself.

Maybe they'd had a fight. Maybe there'd been an accident.

Or maybe the threat wasn't a physical one. Maybe this mistress had been a little more special to Alistair than the others. Special enough to threaten to leave Emily for?

Such things weren't really done in those days, and the virtuous Alistair would never have allowed the world to know that he'd not only cheated on the mother of his child, but dumped her for a much younger woman.

So maybe the threat was physical, after all. Maybe Alistair, or Rose, or both of them, were plotting to kill Emily. Maybe she just got to them before they got to her.

It was getting late, but before I went to bed I managed to ferret out a picture from those society pages I mentioned, taken the night 1913 became 1914, just a few months after the first Baird ball.

It was old and grainy, and I couldn't tell much about the short, slim girl smiling at her cousin-in-law's side. She looked pretty enough—her eyes were enormous, in that good way—but not so much that it would shock you if you saw her on the street.

I thought there was something familiar about her triangular face, the line of her mouth. Maybe I'd seen the lower half of her face in the picture of the Baird ball. Unfortunately, I'd given that back to Snick already. He didn't like having it out of the house, and besides, he'd been right: the guests' faces were mostly covered, and I hadn't found much value in studying chins.

I dreamt about Baird House all night long, about Snick and Rebecca, Tristan and his Frenchies, Elaine and Phil Mendoza, Mrs. B and her enthusiasm. Neither Percy nor Clifford were there, not until the rest of us sat down to dinner and were served both their heads, each complete with the proverbial apple in the mouth and leafy garnish. Mrs. B exclaimed at length about how *gorgeous*—Just *gorgeous!*—they were.

In the end, I was alone in the house. Even Plant was gone. I felt vulnerable without him, in that way I'd felt vulnerable alone in my own house in the days before I got him. I walked from room to room, looking for him, while rain battered the windows. The sound got louder and louder, drowning out my calls for Plant, until I realized it was more than just rain. There was banging, creaking—and then cracking.

The rhododendron vines burst through the

windows, flowing and winding themselves around everything. The furniture, the light fixtures, the walls.

Strangling it all. They would strangle me next.

～

Thankfully, I woke up before that whole strangulation thing came to fruition. I took a shower, then dragged Plant out of bed, rushing his walk not because I was late, but because I was eager to get to the shop. Gretchen and Noah wouldn't be in until after ten, and in the meantime, there didn't tend to be a lot of customers in a pet store at seven in the morning. I would almost certainly have a lot of spare time to study Emily's middle journal.

As soon as I was ensconced on my stool beside the register, I flipped through the pages until I came back to the one about cutting the roses. I tilted my head, reading the words again. *Cutting* the roses, not *clipping* them or *trimming* them. I had no doubt the choice was a deliberate one. Emily Baird was into her code words, and I meant to crack every one.

There was a sketch beneath the little rose-cutting anecdote, drawn in Emily's always crude hand. I wondered whether that was part of the code, too. Maybe she was actually a fantastic artist, and just didn't want to draw anything so clearly that somebody other than her could decipher it. I squinted at the crooked lines, the jagged edges of ... was that a tree?

I was pretty sure it was. I hadn't recognized it at first because it was drawn the wrong way. On its side, with the branches pointing left and the roots pointing right. I tilted my head to look at the thing beside it, and decided it might be an axe. A poorly proportioned one—it was as big as the tree's main branches—but an axe nonetheless.

Which was weird, because Emily hadn't cut down a tree, she'd cut down a rose bush. Or so she said.

Unless she'd cut down both. Struck with several realizations at once, I flipped back through the journal, faster and faster, my eyes darting to every sketch. And when I'd looked at them all, I looked at them again.

The other two books were still up in my apartment. I'd need them to be sure, especially the last one that was almost all sketches. But I thought, in fact I was almost certain, that—

"Hello?"

With a little cry of surprise that made Plant bark (and embarrassed me thoroughly), I looked up to find a woman who could have been Paisley Grant's sister standing at the counter, glaring at me.

"I'm so sorry," I said. "How long were you standing there?"

"Long enough to know you aren't doing much for Gretchen."

"I'm so sorry," I said again, ringing up her bag of cat food.

"Maybe you should get a bell or something. Do you know who I am?"

I looked up at her, hoping my horror didn't show in my face. She *wasn't* Paisley Grant's sister, was she? But no, she couldn't have been. None of the Grants would know Gretchen's name. "I'm sorry, I ..."

She laughed, as if she'd been teasing me all along. "It's okay, I'm not a celebrity or anything. Or a Baird, which in this town is better than a celebrity, right? I just thought, maybe gossip. I've certainly heard the gossip about *you*."

Fizzing. I gave her the smallest smile I reasonably could without being unforgivably rude.

She shrugged. "I was the Bairds' PA before you."

"You're Simone?" It just sort of popped out, before I could really check my tone. I gaped at her, my first thought that I couldn't believe Percy had been worried about me getting harassed, if this was Clifford's type. Percy's type too, maybe, considering the resemblance to Paisley. He'd called me pretty, that night we met, but if this lady was his idea of the word, I couldn't say I qualified.

"So yes, you have heard the gossip." Simone sighed, although she didn't look all that upset. "I cannot wait to leave this town."

"But you haven't," I said.

"Not until P's trial is over. I have to testify, obviously, about Cliff's whereabouts that afternoon, and his state of mind. Mrs. B is going to throw a *fit*, having to look at me in court. How is P, by the way? Have you heard anything?"

I was unreasonably annoyed by her referring to Percy only by his first initial. "No."

"Do you really think he did it?"

"No. Do you?"

"Not a bit."

All right then. Maybe she wasn't all bad. Although as

I saw it, anybody who would be with not only a married man, but with Clifford Baird, couldn't be much good either. "But I guess there's not much you can say that will help him. All you did was have lunch with Clifford, right?"

"Right. And before you or whoever you tell this story to asks, yes, we left the restaurant separately, and yes, there are witnesses that can corroborate that. I went to a meeting right after, which I can also corroborate."

"Oh. I wasn't …"

She waved a hand. "Of course you were. So how come you're not working at Tybryd?"

"Why would I be?"

"That's where P ships the PAs off to, when he's afraid they'll sue if they get fired outright. I do event planning there."

I wasn't sure what to say to that, so I just told her her total. She put her card into the chip reader and said, "Guess he's not afraid you'll sue. Maybe you should be afraid he'll sue *you*."

Well, that ended the whole encounter on a bit of a sour note. As if the interruption hadn't been bad enough. All lowlight, no highlight there.

Ignoring the fact that the "interruption" had been to do the job for which I was being paid, I went back to Emily's journal just as soon as the door closed behind Simone.

There were a lot of sketches that I was pretty sure were supposed to be trees.

I was also pretty sure the ones with branches, as

opposed to the triangle-shaped evergreens, represented Alistair.

All of those, except the one on the rose-cutting page, were standing.

So Emily had cut Alistair down with the roses. And if she'd killed both her husband and his mistress … and if Clifford's death was meant to mirror Alistair's …

The woman who'd just walked out of here might just be in big trouble.

Chapter Sixteen

I MANAGED to get an appointment with Ruby first thing the next morning. Knowing her patience to be limited, I didn't bore her with every detail of what I'd found in, and deduced from, Emily's journals. But I gave her the highlights, which as I saw it were as follows:

Rose was Alistair's mistress. Rose disappeared sometime after January of 1914. Alistair died in February of 1915. And Emily almost certainly killed them both.

I did not mention Mrs. B. True, if I was looking for a straightforward parallel, she was the obvious suspect in Clifford's murder. She'd spoken of Emily with some admiration, and she'd had access to the journals for years. She could very well have found all the same things I did, and decided to follow Emily's footsteps right to the edge of Adley Falls. I was no longer as certain as I'd once been that Bessie Baird didn't have the grit to kill her husband.

But I was pretty sure she would never deliberately frame Percy for it.

And anyway, I'd gotten enough Bairds arrested lately.

Ruby could make that connection herself, if she wanted to.

Which she did not. In fact, she didn't take anything I said all that seriously. She seemed to think it took an awful lot of leaps in logic to get to murder from a couple of sentences about gardening and a few bad sketches.

"But if Alistair and his mistress were killed around the same time, you can see how that would put Simone Benoit in danger," I pressed. "You'll at least keep an eye on her, right?"

Ruby said she would. I suspected she meant it in the general sense in which her department kept an eye on every citizen of Bryd Hollow, but there wasn't much more I could do. Besides, Simone was a witness in the trial of a wealthy and powerful man. Surely that warranted keeping a little extra watch over her, regardless. I was sure she would be fine.

Pretty sure. As long as she didn't go hiking.

As I was about to leave the police station, my concerns for Simone's fate gave way to a more immediate concern for Plant's; I could hear him barking outside, and it was not his nice bark. I rushed for the exit, and nearly repeated my Bryd Hollow debut performance of getting smacked with a door by a ratbag. Not that I knew he was a ratbag right at that exact moment, but I was to find out in a matter of seconds.

Thankfully this door was glass, and I saw the middle-aged, pot-bellied man coming in time to jump out of the way. He didn't even glance at me, much less apologize, as he stormed into the station and started bellowing.

"Whose dog is that?" he wanted to know. "Who left a

rabid pit bull in the parking lot? It attacked me! I want to press charges!"

"Odsbodikins, not every dog with a square head is a pit bull!" This was a pet peeve of mine, and for a second it distracted me from the rest. "He is not a pit bull. He looks nothing like a pit bull."

"That's your dog?" He looked me up and down. "A *woman* has no business keeping a dangerous dog like that. You obviously can't control it. You're not even big enough to handle it."

I crossed my arms, mostly to keep them from smacking the guy without my say-so. Another peeve: people referring to dogs as *it*. "*He* is not dangerous, and I can handle him just fine."

"Problem here, Mr. Baumgartner?" Ruby, no doubt drawn by the commotion, had come out of her office. I noticed the three other officers in the room were all watching us with varying degrees of amusement on their faces, and no apparent intention to intervene.

"Yes, there is!" the man apparently called Baumgartner said. "Her dog attacked me. I want to press charges."

Ruby looked at me. "Plant's in your car?"

"Yes, it's my day off, and we were going to go for a little hike after." I lifted my chin. "It's cold, and it's not even sunny. I left the windows cracked, obviously."

She waved that away. "I'm not questioning your responsibility as a dog owner."

"Well I am!" said Baumgartner. "That dog attacked me! I just told you!"

"All right"—Ruby put a hand on each of our shoulders—"both of you, outside."

I saw the problem as soon as we got to the lot. Ratbag Baumgartner had parked his price-of-a-small-house SUV so close to my car, I wouldn't have been able to open the passenger side door, had I had a two-legged passenger to worry about.

"Well of course he's going to bark at you, if you park that close." I gave him a disgusted look as I opened the rear door on the driver's side for Plant, who was once again barking.

Baumgartner jumped back like I'd just tossed a bomb onto the pavement. "Don't let it out!"

I rolled my eyes, which I'll allow was pretty rude. I was generally sympathetic when people were afraid of dogs, but this guy had shredded my last nerve. "Plant, sit."

Plant immediately quieted and sat. (Much to my relief, because that really could've gone either way.)

"Looks like he's under her control to me," said Ruby.

"But she wasn't here, was she?" Baumgartner tossed his hand back toward my car. "And that window is not *cracked*. It's open enough for the pit bull to get its head out and snap at me."

"Not a pit bull," I said, "and I can guarantee he did no such thing. He'll bark or growl if he's baited, but he would not snap at a human." I turned to Ruby. "My guess is, Mr. Baumgartner here got scared when Plant started barking. But he doesn't want to admit that, so he exaggerated it into something that would justify his anger."

Baumgartner started to protest (in some not-nice language), but closed his mouth and moved when I walked Plant past him.

"Like I said, obviously he was going to bark when you parked this close to his car." I sidled between the cars to have a look at the passenger side.

"And you *dented* it!" I looked from Baumgartner to Ruby and back again, pointing at the dent in question. "You hit my car with your door! And you what? Expected my dog to just shut up about it?"

Baumgartner sneered at my car. "That was already there."

"It most certainly was not."

He gave me a patronizing look that made me want to sic Plant on him right then and there. "Sweetheart, that's a piece of junk. The whole thing is worth less than my tires."

"Okay." Ruby came to stand between us, hands on her hips. "Mr. Baumgartner, a dog attack needs to be a physical thing. Barking at you is not a crime."

"It was physical! I told you, it snapped at me!"

"Can you show me a bite, or any damage to your clothing?"

He pressed his mouth closed.

"Well then, I'm afraid I have nothing to go on there." Ruby looked back at me. "Do you want to file an accident report for the dent?"

"Now you're going to let *her* file a report against *me*?" Baumgartner got right up in Ruby's face. "Is this some kind of girl power thing? Ganging up on me?"

Ruby was apparently as far out at the end of her rope as I was, because she just tossed her hands. *"Really?"*

"Don't think I don't know what you're doing!" Baumgartner jabbed his finger at her. "Calling me down here to get attacked by a pit bull!"

"Not a pit bull," I said through my teeth, but they both ignored me.

"This really is low, even for you," he went on. "I'll have you fired this time! You have nothing on me and you know it, but you continue to harass me. I've already called my lawyer, you know. He's meeting me here!"

I had to turn away so he wouldn't see how desperately I was trying not to laugh at that. It was just so much like a little boy telling a schoolyard rival that his big bad older brother would be there any second.

Ruby started talking, but I wasn't listening anymore. As it happened, I'd turned toward the windshield of Mr. Baumgartner's car.

Where I saw a little square sticker that was even more interesting than this whole kerfuffle.

It was a JoraLab parking sticker.

∼

"I told Snick you would be my Watson." I pushed Plant's paw off my shoulder for at least the half-dozenth time.

He huffed in my ear.

"Look, this is detecting, buddy. It's not always glamorous."

I was still in my car, in the parking lot at the police

station. Ruby and Baumgartner had gone inside after I declined to file an accident report for the dent. I couldn't *prove* the ratbag had done it, after all, and it was only a little ding (in what I had to admit had been accurately described by the ratbag himself as a piece of junk). I had more important things to get to.

Like looking at JoraLab's website on my phone, which was what I'd spent the past ten minutes doing. Plant had spent the latter six of those minutes smacking my shoulder to let me know I was very boring.

I couldn't find Baumgartner's name or picture, which meant he wasn't high up in the company, despite his expensive car. Who was he? And what did Ruby want with him? He'd mentioned her harassing him repeatedly.

So Ruby had taken me seriously when I told her about the disposable phone. She was looking into JoraLab for some reason.

But this wasn't an active investigation anymore, was it? She'd already made an arrest, which as I understood from my vast experience watching TV meant that it was in the district attorney's hands now.

Okay, so this was about the trial. Either the DA or Ruby, or both, thought Baumgartner knew something that could help them prosecute Percy.

What? And how did it relate to my theories about Clifford and Alistair, and Emily and Rose, and maybe even Simone? If there were mistresses and uncertain paternity involved, how were they connecting that to Percy?

Crucial questions. Ruby could have answered some of them, but she seemed disinclined to consider me her colleague in this, just because I had no relevant education or experience whatsoever, the snob. And I feared Emily Baird had told me all she could—or would.

I was going to have to strike out on my own, and do some actual modern-day sleuthing.

I started to text Snick, then decided the conversation might be too long for that, and called him instead. "Why is Ruby questioning a JoraLab guy?"

"How would I know this?"

"You live in a house with like a hundred lawyers milling around it every day! You haven't heard anything? Maybe that he's on the witness list for the trial, or something?"

"I don't know that a witness list counts as gossip, and no, I haven't heard anything." Snick sighed into the phone, the sound of a man who knew he was about to regret encouraging me. "How do you know she's questioning this mysterious mad scientist?"

"His name is Baumgartner."

"Frank Baumgartner?"

"Sure. I guess. He looked like he could have been a Frank. I take it you know him?"

"Not really. I think he's only been in Bryd Hollow a few years. He keeps to himself."

"Or nobody wants to go near him." I told him all about my unpleasant encounter with Frank.

"It's good he didn't hit you with the door though," Snick said. "Or maybe it's bad, since maybe he would've died the next day."

"I was thinking the same thing! About him almost hitting me with the door, I mean, like Clifford did.

Not about wishing him dead. What a thing to say, Snick."

He snorted. "Please. As soon as you were alone in your car, you said worse things about him than that."

"Maybe." Obviously. The man had threatened my dog.

"Has it occurred to you that maybe he's just a jerk that Ruby is questioning for some other reason, having nothing to do with Percy's case?" Snick asked. "JoraLab isn't a small employer, it wouldn't be outside the realm of a believable coincidence. This guy could be anyone."

"I'm not sure I find any coincidence believable anymore." I shook my head. Plant threw himself down in the back seat, thoroughly disgusted with both the detective business and me. But I knew I was right. "He's got something to do with this case, and I mean to find out what."

"I like the spirit," said Snick, "but if Ruby won't tell you, and I can't tell you, it seems like you're out of people to ask."

Was I? Maybe not entirely.

I started my car.

Chapter Seventeen

I COULD HAVE CALLED, but I was hoping Simone would be more friendly if I went there in person, bearing some cat toys that Gretchen had put on the clearance shelf. I'll admit it wasn't the best offer, but I wasn't in much of a financial position for good bribes.

It's hard to explain Tybryd, if you've never seen it. Just the *scale* of it, and all topped with that red roof. The giant ferris wheel off to one side, almost as much of a landmark as the manor itself. The grounds were famous too, boasting half a dozen separate gardens (not to mention a small vineyard), each with its own rare plants and unique features. And of course, no grand estate was complete without a hedge maze.

It didn't look like a house, or a castle, or even the hotel it had become. It was its own thing. And it was breathtaking.

Much as I'd done with town, I tried to imagine it as Emily would have seen it. What had it been like, to go up that drive for the first time? Had she come when the rhododendrons were in bloom? The ferris wheel wouldn't have been there, or some of the outbuildings. But the house itself hadn't changed very much, not on the outside.

And they probably had some of her things on display inside. I wished I were there for fun, so I could take a few hours and explore the place. But fun wasn't in the cards for me. I doubted Percy was having much fun.

So as not to disturb the view, they'd put all the parking out back, mostly underground. As with Baird House, stone gargoyles and ravens kept watch over me as I drove around the main building and found a spot in the crowded garage. Then I grabbed my pathetic offering of loot and went inside (alone, I'd dropped Plant at home) to tell the concierge I wanted to speak with Simone about possibly holding my wedding there.

It didn't occur to me until that moment that a place this size probably had more than one event planner, and that maybe Simone wouldn't even be there. Luckily, she was. Her eyes went wide when she saw me, but her greeting was generic and professional.

She led me through the opulent lobby and down the equally opulent main hallway, to an elegant office that might once have been a drawing room. It looked like it was shared, but once again my luck held: nobody else was there now.

"Are you really engaged?" she asked as she closed the door.

"No. Do you really think Percy is innocent?"

"Haven't we covered this?"

"Yes, but I wanted to make sure. I thought you'd be more likely to help me, if you were on his side."

"I didn't say I was on his side, I just said I didn't think he did it. What've you got in the bag?"

"Some cat toys. And a bed." I held my wrinkled fabric grocery bag out to her. "They're for you."

"You're trying to bribe me with cat toys?" Despite the skepticism in her voice, she took the bag. Her nails were bright, and perfectly manicured.

Self-conscious about my own chewed-upon thumbs, I stuffed my hands into the pockets of my coat. "I also might have some information you'd be interested in. You're not … by any chance …"

I cleared my throat. I did want to warn her that if she was pregnant, there might be trouble coming her way. But it was going to be embarrassing if I had to explain the convoluted route by which I'd formed this theory. Ruby certainly thought it was nuts. "You're not involved in any kind of … paternity … thing … with the Bairds, are you?"

"Paternity thing?" Simone set the bag of cat stuff down on the floor next to one of the desks and sat, gesturing for me to take the nearest chair. "Are you asking if I'm pregnant?"

"Kind of?"

"No. And it was long over between me and Cliff, you know. That's the irony, I broke it off way before I got fired for it. Sorry, I mean"—she made finger quotes in the air—"transferred."

"But you had lunch with him," I said as I sat down.

She shrugged. "People have lunch. We were friends."

"Do you know if he was seeing anybody else?" *Anybody he might have impregnated?*

"He wasn't. He was hitting on me at that lunch. I came close to slapping him for it."

"I'm not sure him hitting on you means he wasn't seeing anybody else, considering he was a cheater."

"He only cheated on his wife. He kept his girlfriends to one at a time."

I considered her, and decided she was telling the truth, if for no other reason than she didn't seem like the type to lie out of shame or embarrassment. Or the type to feel shame or embarrassment. "Is there any reason any of the Bairds might *think* you're pregnant? Or even that you were still involved with Clifford when he died?"

"No, and probably not."

Odsbodikins. There went my leverage, if she and Clifford really had been well and truly over. "Okay. Never mind, then. The information I mentioned probably wouldn't be of use to you."

"So it's just the cat toys?"

"And a bed!"

"Hope you don't want anything too big, then."

"Nothing big at all. I just want to know what Frank Baumgartner has to do with the case against Percy."

"What makes you think I would know stuff about the case?" Simone's tone hadn't changed, but her face had gotten cagey. She might as well have been wearing a t-shirt that said *I know stuff about the case.*

"You said you were testifying," I said. "The district attorney hasn't—"

"Sat each witness down to discuss the other witnesses? No, they don't do that."

"So Frank is a witness?"

She picked up a pen from her desk and started nibbling at the cap. See what I mean? Cagey. "Either he is, or they want him to be," she said finally. "I've seen him at the DA's office a couple of times, but he doesn't seem super agreeable."

"He works for JoraLab."

"Interesting."

"Is it?"

"Not really. I was just being polite."

I crossed my arms. "I don't believe you. I think you know more about Frank than you're letting on."

"What makes you think that?"

"You look cagey."

"I am cagey. I was Clifford Baird's mistress. Scarlet women are always cagey."

"This was particularly cagey." I bit my lip. I hadn't gotten a good read on Simone. Given her affinity with Clifford, I was pretty sure I could rule out her being a woman of great character. But she was smart, and funny, and most importantly for my present needs, blunt. She didn't strike me as somebody who *liked* being cagey. She struck me as somebody who preferred laying things right out.

I decided my best chance at getting her help was to do the same. "Simone, here's the thing. I gave evidence to the police that contributed to Percy's arrest."

"I know."

"Right, I know you do, but I was going somewhere with that."

"Which was where?"

"I can't *stand* it!" I blurted. I probably sounded like Mrs. B. The exclamation point in my tone was very clear. "He didn't do it, and he's going on trial partly because of me, and that is *not okay*! And I think I might be on to something, some things, some new evidence that might help clear his name. But it's kind of ... circumstantial. And also over a century old. So Ruby won't help me pursue it, and I have to give her something concrete to get her on my side, and—"

"All right, all right." Simone made a downward gesture with her hand, like she was telling a small child to use their indoor voice. "Calm down, Daphne Doo."

"Did you just call me Daphne Doo?"

"Yeah. Like the cartoon." She gestured at me. "That's the look you're going for, no? Cute little detective girl?"

"That's not their last name, you know. It's not like they're one big family and Scooby Doo is their dad."

"Of course not, Fred would obviously be the dad." Simone started chewing on the pen again, and regarded me through narrowed eyes. "I guess it's nice you're trying to help P. We didn't get along so great at the end, for obvious reasons, but he's not a bad guy overall. And he doesn't deserve this."

"No, he doesn't."

She sighed. "Fine. I guess this isn't a secret, it'll probably come out at the trial anyway. Sandy who works at the DA's office—you wouldn't know her, she doesn't live in Bryd Hollow—but she's a friend of mine. We were out for drinks last week and I asked her about it, because Frank was being so aggressive when I ran into him at the office. She says they made some connection or other between Cliff and JoraLab, but the evidence was lost."

I swallowed, and offered no explanation for the lost evidence.

Simone didn't seem to notice my guilty look, and went on talking. "But then a little while ago our man Frank starts spending money. Like a lot of it. Gets a flashy car, that kind of thing. No explanation, no clear place such a windfall could have come from. So they start thinking maybe he did some work for Cliff on the side, or something."

"Like Clifford bribed him?"

"With something better than cat toys."

I fidgeted with the sleeve of my coat, pondering this. "Do you know what they're going to have you testify about? Is it only about that day, or is there any family stuff, since you lived in the house?"

"They'll definitely get it on the record that P and Cliff fought a lot. And that P resented being forced into a marriage he didn't want." Simone gave me a slow smile. "That'll make Miss Paisley good and mad. I hope she's there."

Not that I wanted to bond with Clifford's mistress or anything, but I couldn't help but smile back at the thought. "Anything that might relate to paternity, or anything like that?"

She cocked her head at me. "That's why you asked if I'm pregnant. You're thinking Cliff paid this guy to rig a paternity test?"

"Maybe?"

"And you're thinking the DA is going to try to suggest, what, that maybe P isn't really Cliff's kid?"

"Or that Clifford was going to *claim* Percy wasn't his kid, as a way to disinherit him that couldn't be challenged. I don't think that's actually what happened," I hastened to add, "only that the DA might try to go that route. It could make Percy look guilty."

Sadly, I had no alternative explanation whatsoever for what *had* actually happened. I couldn't put any of this together in any kind of form that made sense.

Simone scoffed. "They'd never get away with that. P is so clearly Cliff's kid. Have you *seen* the dimples?"

"I have." I sighed, for a number of reasons. "Well, thank you. You've been a big help."

"I'm guessing not big enough," she said. "You've only got a few days, you know, if you really think you can help P's case."

"What?" I frowned as I got to my feet. "The trial doesn't start until after Thanksgiving."

"That's the old schedule. They just moved it up again."

"What?" I repeated, my stomach sinking. "Why?"

"If you'd been to the county courthouse lately, you wouldn't have to ask. It's going to be a circus until this is over. I guess they just want to put it behind them before the true crime TV crews take up permanent residence."

"So when you say a few days, you mean …?" I could hear my pulse in my ears, muffling Simone's voice a little as she answered.

"Jury selection starts Monday."

This was not good. Not one bit of it.

I paced back and forth across my apartment, chewing at my nails, making Plant nervous with my nervousness. Just waiting until it was time to close the pet shop.

So I could do what, exactly?

Monday. Jury selection starts Monday.

It was Thursday.

I couldn't solve this crime in three days. How could I possibly solve this crime in three days?

And over a weekend, no less?

He's going to jail.

My accusing inner voice was right, wasn't it? An innocent man (whose dimples were not the point) was going to go to jail. Because of a phone, and a murderer who was also a dirty framer.

And also because of me.

Three days to fix it.

I didn't even know where to look anymore. I'd left Tybryd more confused than I was when I got there.

Well, what had I expected? That Simone, who was apparently only tangentially related to whatever really happened to Clifford Baird, would be able to just lay it all out for me? She couldn't hand me the answers any more than anybody else could.

Or almost anybody else.

There was one ...

Three days.

Time was running out. Not even running; time *was*

out. Or up. Whatever you called it when there was no more time.

No more to spend on trying to solve old riddles. No more to spend on thinking things through.

And no more to spare for beating around the bush.

I could either accept that I was at a dead end (which was not acceptable), or I could accept that if I wanted to know the story with Frank Baumgartner, I was going to have to get it straight from him.

And I was pretty sure he wasn't going to give it to me willingly.

Chapter Eighteen

LET me just say up front that I am not proud of what I did next. I mean, when I look back on it, I do sometimes giggle. But I'm definitely not proud.

I just didn't feel like I had a lot of options. Frank Baumgartner was clearly the rattiest of ratbags, and I had zero time to let him choose whether or not to help me, when I knew perfectly well which route he'd take.

Anyway, judge me if you will. I certainly judged myself, when things got bad. But I'd do it all again.

It wasn't hard to find Frank's address, now that I knew his full name. The fact that he was a Bryd Hollow resident was probably why Clifford had chosen him, of all the employees of JoraLab, to pull into whatever conspiracy was afoot.

I drove over as soon as I was done closing the shop, to a dismal little row house on a dismal little street in the less picturesque part of town. Apparently Frank hadn't gotten around to spending Clifford's money on a fancy house, but his luxury SUV was parked right out front. He was home.

Good.

I wasn't sure how we would get in if he was the kind of guy who locked his door even when he was inside. He wouldn't just offer us a warm welcome and a cup of tea if I knocked. And I suspected Plant wouldn't be great at climbing through windows, especially if he was required to do it with stealth.

Not that I wanted anybody to do any window climbing, anyway. I definitely did not want to break into Frank Baumgartner's house. I wanted plausible deniability here. I was coming by for a visit, that was all, and happened to find the door unlocked.

If the door wasn't unlocked, maybe I would just scrap the whole idea. Or maybe I would knock, after all, and do the whole thing from his porch if I had to. That might even give me more plausible deniability; if a witness happened to see the whole thing, it probably wouldn't look quite the same to them as it would look to Frank.

I also wasn't sure what I would do if Frank owned a gun. And carried it on him. This was the South; plenty of people did.

Okay, so my plan wasn't all that well formed. But the basic underlying principles were solid: One, Frank was clearly afraid of big, blockheaded dogs like mine. And two, my blockhead could be particularly scary, if I wanted him to.

As I've mentioned, Plant had some skills. He rarely used them, but he had them. He'd been a gift from my parents, in those dark days after the shooting when I was terrified of being alone, but refused to become that girl who lives with her parents because she's terrified of being alone. So a big watchdog was the compromise, and they paid for Plant's fancy, expensive watchdog training.

But we'd never used it in a formal, official way. As in, in a situation where watchdogging was actually required. We'd never had a reason to.

Suppose he'd forgotten some of the commands? Or just, you know, ignored me because he saw a fun napkin?

Feeling less and less like this was a good idea, I made Plant stop to pee, then walked around to Frank's kitchen door, and turned the knob.

It opened.

I walked right on in.

Frank was sitting on an unfortunate plaid couch, watching TV and, by the smell of it, eating something drenched in gravy. The couch faced away from the kitchen, so he didn't even realize we'd come in until I said, as forcefully as I could, "Plant, *hold*!"

Bless my boy, he barked once, then immediately ran around to the front of the couch, where he dropped into a crouch and bared his teeth at Frank Baumgartner. It probably helped that he didn't much like the guy.

Frank sat there and stared, his mouth a wide *O*, like he couldn't quite work out what had just happened. (Well honestly, Frank, learn to lock your door. It's amazing how confident and comfortable men can be conditioned to be. You'd never catch a woman sitting with her back to an unlocked door.) He held a plate of what might have been a microwave dinner. A brown blotch on his white sleeveless t-shirt suggested he'd spilled some.

"Hi, Frank!" I smiled at him. "Here's the thing. You were totally right today about Ruby. She can't really *make* you answer her questions, can she? But Plant here doesn't know much about legal rules or your right to an attorney or whatever. He can make you do whatever he wants."

Frank's eyes shifted from Plant to me, his face turning beet red. He set his plate down on the cushion beside him and started to get up. "You b—"

Plant interrupted both the word and the movement with another bark, and a growl that I could completely see being scary, if you'd never seen him prance around like the goofball he was. He crept a little closer to Frank's feet, but not close enough for Frank to kick him.

Frank shrank back. All that blood that had rushed to his face left again in a hurry, and he turned sort of gray.

Maybe this is a good time to reiterate that I recognize it's unkind to use a dog to threaten a person who's afraid of dogs. Worse than unkind. You might even call it unconscionable.

But I also want to stress that Frank was in no actual danger. *Hold* was exactly what it sounded like: Plant was supposed to hold the stranger in place and discourage them from moving. If Frank had chosen to move despite that discouragement, he would have been able to. Plant had never even been taught an attack command. I'd insisted from the start that his role be as a deterrent, and only a deterrent; a dog that bit could get into real and serious trouble.

Not that Frank knew any of that. "Call him off," he ground through his teeth.

"Oh, I'll be glad to." I gave him another bright smile. "Just as soon as you tell me why Clifford Baird paid you off. You did a test for him? And what, falsified the results?"

"No. You're wrong."

I sighed. "Plant—"

"About the first part, I mean!" Frank raised his hands, then put them behind him, like I'd tied him up. Which I guessed I sort of had. "He wasn't the one I did the test for." He looked back down at Plant and flicked his tongue over his lips.

"Who did you do the test for, then?" I asked.

"Don't know. I found out later she used a fake name."

"What name?"

"Rose Lake."

Rose. Interesting. "What did she look like?"

"Don't know really. I only met her twice, in coffee shops near my office, and she wore hats and stuff. She was kind of short, I guess. White. Older. Definitely a woman."

"And she asked for a paternity test?"

Frank shook his head. "Not paternity. What she wanted was a little more complicated. She had three samples, and wanted to know if the three people they came from were related at all."

"What three people were they?"

"Her, Clifford Baird, and Percy Baird." He shrugged.

"It wasn't entirely aboveboard, but she paid me to look the other way on a few signatures."

"So you didn't have either Percy or Clifford's consent," I said.

"Technically, no."

"And did you find a relationship between the three?"

"Yes. And that's when I called Clifford."

I crossed my arms. "Because you figured he would pay you even more to double cross your client."

He hesitated, eyes narrowed at me.

I nodded down at Plant. "You were right about him, you know. He can be a very vicious dog. If I tell him to be."

Frank swore, then muttered, very grudgingly, "I fudged the results, yeah." He gave me a look that I guessed was meant to be defiant, but given his weak chin and soft jawline, just came out looking sulky. "But I'm not telling you any more than that. Not that anything I say under duress is going to be admissible anyway, but I'm not implicating myself until I know I'm taken care of. You can tell Ruby I'll make the deal."

"I guess you can tell Ruby yourself."

The trouble with that last bit was, I wasn't the one who'd said it.

I yelped, startled. Plant started barking like crazy. Frank laughed and laughed.

And Ruby Walker, emerging from the kitchen with her hands on her hips, rolled her eyes at me. *"Seriously?"*

So much for a woman being too smart to have her back to an unlocked door. Had I been a little smarter (or even a little smart), at least I'd have had some warning, and Ruby might have found me in a less incriminating position.

Even better if I'd made Frank give me his phone, or put his hands up, or something that would have kept him from hitting the emergency SOS button. Which was what he'd done to get Ruby there.

I wasn't a very good criminal.

Hence my being in the back of a police car. *Cuffed*. Ruby sure seemed to like cuffing people who were not actually a danger to anybody. But maybe she considered me a flight risk, since she'd just left me here while she talked to Frank inside.

At least she'd let Plant in back with me. I'd have to call Gretchen to get him, if I was going to jail.

Or not. I'd been sitting there for maybe fifteen or twenty minutes, Ruby still inside Frank's house, when a van pulled up across the street. A van with four nauseating words on the side.

Buchanan County Animal Control.

What was this? They weren't taking *Plant* to jail?

I swallowed hard as my stomach turned. No. They couldn't. How could they? I'd made good and sure that Plant hadn't done anything wrong. He hadn't even gotten close enough to Frank to drool on him. Looking scary wasn't a crime; that was just Frank's interpretation. The overreaction of a man who was afraid of dogs.

Taking advantage of that overreaction to intimidate

somebody was the crime here, and I was the only one who'd done that.

Right?

Apparently not. Ruby came out of Frank's house, talked to the animal control officer, and gestured at her car.

The animal control officer opened the door on the opposite side from me, the side Plant was on. And picked up the end of my boy's leash.

I couldn't do anything to stop him, not with those stupid handcuffs on. Maybe that was why she'd cuffed me. I just sort of leaned into Plant, like maybe my weight would hold him back. "What are you doing? Where are you taking him? He didn't do anything wrong! If it's just because Ruby needs to take me somewhere, I can call somebody to pick him up. You guys don't have to worry about him."

The animal control officer was ignoring my babbling, so I threw myself over Plant's body to shout out the open door at Ruby. "I can have somebody here to get him in five minutes. Five minutes!"

Ruby didn't say anything either.

By this point, Plant was good and nervous. The whole situation was weird enough, and now I was yelling and, yeah, okay, crying a little. Plant hated when people cried, especially me. His hackles had gone up. When the officer gave the leash a little tug to encourage him out of the car, he gave the guy a low growl in return.

The guy unwisely ignored this warning, and tugged on the leash again. Plant started barking his head off. It was his scariest bark.

The officer slammed the door closed and came around to talk to me through the open window on my side. Plant tried to lunge, but I twisted my back and blocked him with my shoulders.

"Ma'am, you're upsetting the dog," the officer called over Plant's continued hysterics. "If you can't calm down, and calm him down, I'm going to have to get the control pole. That'll make things a lot more stressful for all of us."

"Things?" I was definitely not calming down. "What things? What are you doing with him?"

Ruby stuck her head in the window alongside the officer's. Plant calmed down a little, in the sense that he wasn't trying to climb over me to get to her the way he had with the other guy. At least he knew this one. But he was still making a lot of noise.

"What did you expect, Minerva?" Ruby tossed her hands. "You broke into a man's house—"

"*Walked* in. The door was open."

"—and *attacked* him with your dog."

"I didn't attack anybody, and neither did Plant! He never came into contact with Frank in any way!"

Ruby ignored my interruptions. "Obviously Plant has to be treated as a dangerous animal at this point. This nice animal control officer is going to remove him from your care until we get this straightened out."

I was every bit as hysterical as Plant, and crying freely. Which was a shame, because my nose was starting to run, and I had no hands free. "Fine, if he can't be in my care, and obviously he can't because I'm in blasted handcuffs, why can't I call Gretchen? Can't she vouch for him and take custody of him, or whatever?"

"That's not how this works." Ruby's voice might have been slightly sympathetic. Not that that helped me any. She gave me the over-the-glasses-stare. "This is happening, one way or the other. Plant will be fine at the county shelter for now. Nobody's going to hurt him, I promise. But Officer Wilkes here is right: if you can't help us calm him down, this is going to cause him a lot of stress."

This is happening, one way or the other.

I repeated the phrase in my mind, once, twice. A third time. My heart sank, my hands shook. But none of that mattered. Nothing I could do right now would matter.

So better the one way than the other. I took several deep, gulping breaths and turned to my dog. "Plant, settle. It's okay. These guys are okay."

I had to say *settle* several more times, in my soothingest voice, but eventually Plant stopped barking. Not that he looked happy about it.

I turned back to Ruby and Officer Wilkes. "Can I be the one to put him in the van?"

They straightened up, giving me a view of their torsos as they exchanged a few quiet words. Then Ruby leaned back down and opened the door. "No. But you can walk alongside Officer Wilkes."

With my encouragement, Plant let Officer Wilkes take his leash, and I walked beside them to the van. The back of it looked like a little moving dog jail. I fought back a fresh wave of tears. Crying would only hurt Plant.

"You'll find a dental bone in my coat pocket," I said to Officer Wilkes. "Would you please hand it to him? He has a routine when I leave him. It'll help."

Officer Wilkes, to my relief, complied with this request. It wasn't a treat-stuffed toy, but at least it would take Plant more than three seconds to devour. With another command from me, Plant hopped up in the back, lay down, and started chewing.

"Be a good boy," I told him, echoing what I said whenever I went out. "I'll be back."

I watched the van doors close on him, and hoped that was true.

Chapter Nineteen

What did you expect, Minerva?

Ruby's words were all I could hear as I paced—uncuffed, finally—around the little room she'd left me in. An interrogation room, I guessed, although the camera in one corner of the ceiling wasn't lit up, and there was no cool two-way mirror like they always had on TV.

At least it wasn't a cell. But it was still the dungeon; we'd gone through that door at the back of the Bryd Hollow Police station, the one they'd taken Percy through the night of his arrest.

I myself had not been arrested—yet. Which was weird, now that I thought of it. Could they cuff you without reading you your rights?

Frank had followed us here, but I hadn't seen him, or even Ruby really, since we arrived. She'd driven me to the station in silence, then just sort of tossed me in this room and left.

As for Plant, he was half an hour away, languishing at

the county shelter. Was he in a cage? He was almost certainly in a cage.

The thing is, and it is an awful thing: you can't explain to dogs. You can't tell them why you're leaving them. They just have to be confused, and wonder.

What did you expect, Minerva?

What, indeed.

I guessed I hadn't expected much of anything, because I obviously hadn't thought this plan through nearly enough. Maybe not even enough for it to qualify as a plan. Maybe there hadn't been any thoughts at all rolling around in my nitwitted head.

Also obvious: I'd gone too far. Way too far.

And I didn't mind that for myself. I certainly didn't mind it for Frank Baumgartner. But putting Plant in danger had never been part of the not-even-good-enough-to-call-it-a-plan plan.

How much danger were we talking?

My ribcage closed around my heart and lungs. It was hard to breathe.

They couldn't put him down, surely. They couldn't do *that*. He hadn't bitten anybody. He hadn't caused the least bit of actual harm.

I flopped into the folding chair on one side of the table and buried my head in my hands, giving in to more tears. A couple hours earlier I would have said the very thought of Plant being destroyed as a dangerous dog was ridiculous. Utterly impossible.

But a couple hours earlier I also would have said it was impossible for him to get in trouble at all. I'd thought I was so clever, making sure he didn't actually *do* anything. But I wasn't clever. Not even a little.

I began to see how somebody could be driven to murder. If Frank Baumgartner got my dog killed, or taken away from me, I might have to push *him* off a cliff.

Ruby had taken my phone (I didn't know whether or not that was legal, but it had seemed a bad time to ask), so I had no clock by which to judge how long I sat alone in that room, despising myself and Frank in roughly equal measure. If only there'd been one of those two-way mirrors I mentioned, I might have been able to estimate based on how many of my hairs turned gray while I was in there.

At last, after hours or years or several lifetimes, Ruby came in. I immediately jumped up and started asking about Plant, but she flopped a hand around, like she was swatting away an annoying bug, and said, "Zip it!"

I guessed I was the bug. I zipped it, and sat when she gestured for me to. She took the chair across from me and stared me down, in silence, for a solid minute.

I had no doubt then, and have no doubt now, that this was just to torture me.

Finally she pried open her disapproval-flattened lips and said, "Here's what happened. You went to visit your friend Frank, just a friendly visit, to chat about Clifford Baird—"

"But that is what happened!" I cut in. Plausible deniability. That was the name of my game. If I could be said to have any game at all, which of course I couldn't. "It's exactly what happened. I mean, not that we're friends. But it was a friendly visit. I just wanted to talk to him, as a concerned citizen. Frank happens to be scared of dogs, so there was a misunderstanding, and it kind of spiraled out of control. But we were just having a conversation, and Plant *didn't do anything wrong*."

Ruby gave me a look that plainly stated she'd been standing in Frank's kitchen long enough to know better. But all she said was, "I'm glad we all see it the same way."

"We all?" Hope rose in my throat. When you're as scared as I was, hope feels a little bit like vomit. "Even Frank?"

"Once he calmed down, yes. His fear, you know, led him to misinterpret things in the moment."

"And he ..." I tilted my head at her. "... spontaneously realized it was a misunderstanding?"

"I helped him to see it."

I knew that must have been the case, but it still surprised me. I decided to be direct about it. "Why would you do that for me? You don't particularly like me, as far as I can tell."

Ruby laughed. "I didn't do it for you. Frank's gone home for now, to get a good night's rest. Tomorrow he's going to drop by the Buchanan County District Attorney's office and discuss being granted immunity for his faulty data handling, in exchange for his testimony in court. *I* only wanted to be sure that testimony was obtained in an entirely aboveboard manner that the defense attorneys could not possibly object to. And what could be more aboveboard than being brought around to seeing the value in sharing the truth, by a good conversation with a friend?"

I blinked at her. Now that I—and more importantly,

Plant—seemed to be out of trouble, the details of my conversation with Frank were starting to seep through my panic a little bit.

But clearly I had some lingering confusion. Surely Ruby wasn't telling me that everything Plant and I had just gone through was going to *help* the case against Percy. Surely she wasn't.

"What do you mean, in court?" I asked. "You aren't dropping the charges? You can't possibly still mean to prosecute Percy."

"You're asking about the DA's job, not mine," said Ruby. "But I see no reason he would drop the charges, no."

"But there was a third party. This woman, who asked for the DNA test in the first place. She—"

"—could have been Elaine," Ruby interrupted. "Or Bessie. Or anyone else involved in a conspiracy to cut Percy out of Clifford's will." She saw I was opening my mouth, and did the whole hand flap thing again. *"Zip it!"*

She stood. "I am not discussing this case with you again. I'll have Roark drive you back over to your car. The county animal shelter is closed for the night, but you can pick up Plant in the morning."

I stared at her, aghast. "What do you mean, closed? Somebody must be there!"

Ruby shook her head. "You really don't know how to quit while you're ahead, do you?"

"But—"

"Minerva! Go home, pick up your dog in the morning—and spend some time between now and then thanking the good lord you aren't wearing an orange jumpsuit."

Well. I supposed she had a point there.

~

I was pretty sure that night was harder on me than it was on Plant. I got to the county shelter fifteen minutes before they opened, and waited in the parking lot until somebody showed up. One small "donation" (which I did not mind making, however meager my funds), and I had my boy back in the car. I fussed over him, and gave him several pieces of cheese. He gave me a couple of licks on the ear, then promptly flopped down and went to sleep.

I opened the pet shop almost an hour late because of it, but I doubted anybody noticed. It was raining, which meant no foot traffic on Honor Avenue, and business was at a crawl. When Gretchen came in just before lunchtime, I gave her a general summary of the prior night's ordeal: that I'd gone to see Frank Baumgartner, to ask him some questions about Percy's case; that we'd had a bit of a clash; that he'd gotten Plant thrown in jail. I left out the parts where I'd been something of a ratbag, myself.

When I asked if I could have the afternoon off, mostly to see if I could use what I'd learned from Frank to help Percy, she was sympathetic to my cause. She loved Percy, of course, and she detested Frank. "Long as you know you won't be paid for those hours," was her only caveat.

"You need to dock me for today anyway. I was late opening, so I could go get Plant."

"Well, that was worth it, wasn't it?" Gretchen bent down to pucker her lips at Plant, who took this as an invitation to slobber all over her face.

Thus freed, I went upstairs to throw a poncho and a few other things into a backpack. Fifteen minutes later Plant and I were back in the car—and on our way to the Adley Falls trailhead.

I needed to think, and therefore I needed a walk. Rain or no rain.

And I still hadn't seen it, the spot where both great-grandfather and great-grandson had met their ends. Not up close.

It was Friday. Jury selection started Monday. The DA was almost certainly going forward with his case. Ruby "Zip It" Walker clearly had no plans to help me—or Percy.

Which meant before the weekend was over, I needed to find Clifford Baird's murderer myself.

"It's all there, Plant," I assured him as I let him out of the car. "It's always there, if you look at it the right way, right? You just have to put it together."

Plant, who was not fond of rain, had no encouragement to offer.

Nor did Tybryd. There was a gate across the trail, with a big fat *No Trespassing* sign attached. *Trail For Guests Only*, declared a smaller sign beneath it.

Naturally, I ignored this. I ducked under the metal and instructed Plant to do the same. Even if we were caught, I doubted adding this small transgression to my list of offenses would move the needle one bit, with regards to the Baird family's opinion of me.

The rain had slowed to a drizzle, but it had already slicked the trail. We didn't pass a soul on the hike up, giving me plenty of time for all that thinking and looking I'd resolved to do. By the time we got to the top, I was thirsty and a little winded ... and I still didn't know who'd killed Clifford.

I sat on a tree stump, and poured some water into a collapsible dog bowl for Plant before taking a drink of my own. Whoever had put up the gate had also tossed up a (probably) hastily and (definitely) haphazardly constructed guardrail, but if I leaned, I could still see through the patchy mist, down to the rushing stream below the falls.

The rocks down there looked jagged. You could see how they would kill a guy.

What had it been like that day, for Emily? Was it sunny? Windy? Cold? Did her ears hurt, the way they do when you stay outdoors too long in the winter? Probably not; she would've had a hat.

Was she nervous?

How did she even convince Alistair to go walking? It was February. And weren't old-timey women presumed to be too delicate for hikes? Maybe she used that delicacy to her advantage; maybe she made some excuse about fresh air and her constitution. Or maybe the two of them made a habit of surveying their domain, like the American royalty they were.

One way or another, she got him up here. He must not have suspected anything. If he'd been on his guard, there would have been a struggle, and she couldn't have won.

So he was relaxed. Maybe he'd even had a couple of drinks first, like Clifford did. No Dramamine in 1915, but there was plenty of alcohol.

No guardrail in 1915, either. She only had to wait until his back was turned, and then just a push …

And what about Clifford? Had he been standing next to the same tree stump I was sitting on? It wasn't a big area; wherever the exact spot was, I couldn't have been more than a step or two away from it.

"Let's just … let's put things in order," I said to Plant. "That should help, right?"

He answered by shaking off the rain and lying down on the leaves that always seem to litter forest floors, whatever the time of year. No opinion, then. I doubted he could even hear me over the noise of the waterfall, which was fine. If anybody else did come up here, they probably wouldn't be able to hear me either.

"September 1913, the first Baird ball. Big-eyed, pointy-chinned Rose is there, and Alistair, and Emily. We don't know whether Alistair's affair with Rose had already begun or not. But it happened somewhere around that time."

Plant put his head between his paws, just in case I'd missed that he was moping. Or possibly disappointed in Alistair Baird's lack of fidelity.

"Fourish months later, January of 1914, Rose's picture is in the paper. Then February of 1915, Emily kills Alistair"—I clapped the stump, catching a dirty look from Plant for my theatrics—"in this very spot. And refers to it as cutting the roses. Which means killing him had something, everything probably, to do with Rose. At some point in there, Rose dies too, or disappears, but we don't know exactly when."

Or disappears.

With those two words, something—and maybe everything—finally clicked.

"Or disappears!" I repeated.

I'd been assuming Rose had disappeared from the records because she died. But in light of recent information, disappearing and living was suddenly a much more interesting possibility.

"Fast forward a couple of generations, and somebody, a woman going by the name of Rose Lake, which we know is a fake name, gives Frank DNA samples from her, Clifford, and Percy. She wants proof they're all related."

I was talking faster and faster now. *"She uses Rose's first name, and wants proof she's a Baird."*

I stood a little too suddenly for Plant's taste, and he sat up, looking around for whatever had gotten me so excited. I started to pace—carefully. The leaves were wet, and it would not do for me to become another casualty of Adley Falls. Certainly not when I was this close to figuring everything out.

"Then Clifford dies—Clifford is *killed*—once again, in this same spot." I swung around to face Plant.

"Then we find out Clifford was thinking about disinheriting somebody. *Then* we find out Clifford paid off Frank to say this Rose person wasn't a Baird!"

I spread my hands, as if that explained everything, but Plant didn't seem to be following me. He was tilting his head from one side to the other, listening for words he knew. (Preferably *home*.)

"So what if Clifford's murder wasn't about *him* having an affair, or about *his* will, or about anybody *he* fathered at all?" I flung my arms wide in triumph. "What if this whole thing is *still about Alistair?*"

Plant thumped his tail.

"See! I knew it! I knew you'd agree with me. She *cut the roses*, right? Cut them off. Cut them *out*. Meaning she made sure they wouldn't get anything, except now one of them wants something! And Clifford wouldn't give it to her, so"—I gestured over my shoulder with my thumb—"off he went."

But who saw him off? That was, of course, the question.

Who was Rose Lake?

Somebody who had access to personal items of the Bairds', that she could use for DNA samples. Hair? Old cotton swabs? I didn't really want to think about the particulars.

Somebody who had access to Clifford's flask, to put some crushed-up Dramamine in there.

Somebody who thought of Dramamine in the first place, which might have meant somebody who knew Percy was an occasional user and had it in his room.

And speaking of framing Percy, somebody who

could have gotten into his office at Tybryd, to plant Clifford's phone in there.

I pulled my own phone out of my pack, and sheltering the screen from the last of the rain with one hand, opened my saved photos and took a long, hard look at Rose Eastridge.

Then I called Carrie.

Chapter Twenty

I was most of the way back down the trail before I made my second call, to Snick. He was less than delighted to hear from me. Especially once he heard what I wanted. In fact, there was an audible huff.

"Not your Watson, remember?" he said. "You promised you weren't going to ask for anything else."

"Actually, I distinctly remember saying I *couldn't* promise that." I stepped gingerly down a slope of wet rocks and guided Plant around it. "Come on, Snick, I just need five minutes."

Another huff. "Fine. But why Sunday morning? That's cutting it kind of close, don't you think?"

Yes, yes I did. I hated the idea of waiting that long. But there were other ideas I hated more. My last confrontation with a desperate, angry, violent woman hadn't turned out all that well.

"That's the soonest you'll be alone in the house," I said. "The family will be at church, and it's Rebecca's day off."

"Normally, yes, but not this weekend. Rebecca's actually coming back Sunday morning."

"Back?" I frowned and stopped, just at the edge of the parking lot. Mine was still the only car in it. "Back from where?"

"I don't know, one of those square states. Friend's wedding."

I started walking again. A lot faster this time. "When does she leave?"

"Half an hour ago. So if you really only need five minutes, you could come now. Percy and Elaine are at work, and Mrs. B has a charity thing. Like *right* now, though. I don't know how long the charity thing goes."

I pushed Plant into the car, then got in myself. "What about Tristan?"

"Tristan left days ago."

"Left? When his brother is about to go on trial for killing his father?" That struck me as a little insensitive, but at least it meant the Frenchies wouldn't be there to give me away.

"Life goes on." I could practically hear the shrug in Snick's voice. "One of the day maids will still be around, but I can sneak you up the old servants' staircase. You know, since none of us servants actually use it."

My jeans were mud-spattered, and a quick glance in the rear-view mirror told me that my hair, already left unwashed that morning in my rush to pick up Plant, had not been improved by the hike. But if this was my opening, it was my opening. It wasn't like it needed to be a dress-up occasion.

I had to go. A lot of conjecture and logical leaps had

gone into my theory, and I had to be sure. One hundred percent, beyond all doubt, hand to my heart *sure*. My evidence was ... whatever was two levels worse than circumstantial, that was what my evidence was. It was going to sound crazy enough to Ruby. I at least needed the strength of my convictions behind me.

"Okay." I looked back at my wet dog, reflecting that he was not, as a rule, a subtle creature. "Plant's not great with sneaking, though. I'm going to drop him at my apartment quick, then I'll be right over."

"As long as quick means quick."

"I'll throw a bone at him and run, I promise."

Which was pretty much what I did. I arrived at Baird House alone shortly afterward, parked illegally on the street, and cut across the grounds (modest, compared to Tybryd's, and thank heavens the Bairds didn't feel they needed a wall). If anybody happened to be watching the security monitors they'd see me, but it was the best I could do. Anyway I could always claim I was just visiting Snick. He was allowed to have visitors, wasn't he?

He opened the backmost door before I could knock, then led me through the wine cellar and up the old, narrow, and excessively creaky servants' staircase. We didn't speak until we got to the top attic, above the staff level even, which the Bairds used for storage.

I hadn't been aware I was holding my breath until Snick closed the attic door behind us. I let it out in a long, slow sigh, blowing my tragic hair out of my eyes. Even if somebody came home, this was a safe place; if anybody came up those caterwauling stairs, we'd know it.

"Where is it?" I asked, but the question wasn't necessary. Snick had already crossed the room to pull a sheet off the enlarged photograph of the 1913 ball, the one that went in the ballroom on the day of the party. It was enormous, and no doubt unwieldy. I wondered how they even got it down the stairs, when the time came.

It was also a high-quality reproduction, significantly digitally enhanced. There was a chance the enhancement made it less accurate, but sharp-and-a-little-off was better than right-on-but-blurry. Compared to the small, grainy images I otherwise had access to, this was the clearest view of Rose I was going to get.

The mask would just be butter upon bacon.

Would she have had the audacity to stand somewhere near Alistair, even in the presence of his wife? The attic had an overhead light, but it was still too dim up there. I turned on my phone's flashlight and leaned forward to examine the guests.

There she was. Two to Alistair's left, so yes, she'd had some cheek.

And some chin.

"See!" I said to Snick, probably a little too loudly considering I was on a secret mission.

"What am I looking at?" he asked.

"Rose Eastridge. Alistair's mistress." I held the photo on my phone up alongside Rose at the ball. "Same chin."

Snick turned his head one way, then the other, much like Plant had done when I was explaining things to him earlier. "You might be right."

"I am right. But that's not all I'm right about. Look." I tapped phone-Rose. "It took me a while to figure it out, because I was looking at her whole face. Her eyes dominate it, so you can't help but see the full picture, and all her other features are totally different."

"Different from what?"

"Different from whom." I pointed back at the ball photo. "But when all you can see is the bottom half of her face—and you can really see it, when it's this big—it's pretty striking."

"Well, nothing's striking me. I have no idea what you're talking about."

I smacked his shoulder, still looking at Rose's half-covered face. "That is *Rebecca's chin*."

For a few seconds, Snick was quiet, as he peered at the photograph. I held my breath again. If he could see it, Ruby would see it. "I guess. So you're saying ... what? Rebecca is related to Rose?"

Then his eyes went wide (with horror or delight, I couldn't have said), and he dropped his voice to a whisper. "You're saying Rebecca killed Clifford? That's why you didn't want her to be here?"

I gestured back at the picture and sat down on a nearby trunk. "I think that confirms it."

Snick clicked his tongue and sucked his breath through his teeth, like I'd just come very close to winning a prize but missed it. "Does it, though? Because I'm going to need a few more blanks filled in."

"Here's what I think happened," I said. "Rose had an affair with Alistair, and got pregnant. She didn't disappear a few months later because she was dead, she disappeared because she ran away and changed her name, probably because her family threw a fit over her expanding belly. That was in 1914. Some time in 1915, Emily found out about the baby."

I stood up again, starting to fidget. "Or Alistair found out about the baby. Percy said he always felt bad about his affairs, I'm sure having a kid on the wrong side of the blanket brought on a whole lot of guilt. So maybe as part of his penance, he decided to recognize the child. But Emily was having none of that, so she killed him before he could make a new will. She *cut the roses*."

Snick leaned against the wall and crossed his arms. "And in your version of this, Rebecca is Rose's ...?"

"Great-granddaughter, maybe?" I shrugged. "I'm not very good at math, but it's been over a century, so she's a few generations on. Carrie once mentioned Rebecca's father dying. Maybe that was when Rebecca found out, and that was the catalyst for coming here."

I turned back to the ball picture, looking at Rebecca's chin on Rose's face, and tried to put myself inside her story. Which was really their story. "So Rebecca starts off at Tybryd to work her way in, and finally manages to insinuate herself into the Baird household, where she steals a couple of DNA samples. She finds Frank, probably because he lives here, and pays him to do a test under the table, which she'll use to threaten Clifford and claim her share of the Baird fortune."

"How's she going to sue Clifford, if she's doing stuff under the table?" asked Snick. "She wouldn't be able to use that in court."

"I didn't say sue him," I pointed out. "I said threaten him. If Clifford doesn't roll over, she figures then she can go to court and try to get a judge to order some admissible tests. But there's no guarantee she could find such a judge, plus that route would take longer, and cost more. So blackmail is easier. Except Frank tips Clifford off, so Clifford knows there's this direct descendent of Alistair out there."

Snick snapped his fingers. "But he doesn't know who it is, because she used a fake name." He seemed to be warming up to my tale as much as I was now.

I nodded. "Exactly. And that makes Clifford nervous. He does his internet searches instead of talking to a lawyer, because he wants to keep it as quiet as possible. He doesn't like what the internet tells him, so he talks to Frank on his secret phone from a soundproofed room, and pays him to alter the results of the test. And Frank tells Rebecca she's not related to Alistair, after all."

"But since Rebecca lives in his house and can spy on him whenever she wants," said Snick, "she finds out that Clifford messed with her test, and it makes her mad enough to kill him?"

"Something like that," I said. "Maybe for revenge, maybe because she just thinks she would have better luck if Clifford were out of the picture and she could go after Mrs. B, or one of the kids. Either way, she calls Clifford—anonymously, she still wouldn't want him to know it's his own chef doing all this—and demands that he meet her at Adley Falls. It's an off time of year, making it a fairly isolated place where they can talk in private, and not be seen. He's a manipulative guy, right, and has a very high and very unearned opinion of his people skills. So he figures he can handle a blackmailer. He agrees to the meeting—and thereby seals his fate."

I made a little *tada* sort of gesture. Story over. And it all fit.

Snick tapped his chin, apparently preparing his critique. "It does have a certain poetry, killing him at the falls."

"Poetic and practical," I said. "She knew it would look like an accident. Especially since she slowed Clifford's reflexes enough to avoid a struggle. But she used Percy's Dramamine for that, just in case the police *didn't* think it was an accident, so she had somebody to frame as a backup plan."

Snick pointed at me. "She used Clifford's phone to frame Percy, too. What, she just picked it out of Clifford's pocket, before she pushed him over?"

"I guess, kind of? She took it at some point, anyway. She wouldn't have wanted it on him, in case they could use it to locate him. The longer it took to find his body, the less likely they'd be to find the Dramamine."

"Well," said Snick, "it's not a *bad* story. But it seems like a lot to get from an old journal."

"Only part of it's from an old journal," I said. "Some of it's from Frank. Some from the flask, some from the Dramamine. Some from Clifford himself."

"Some from your butt."

I sighed. "Some from my butt. But I don't need to prove it. I just need to convince Ruby enough for *her* to prove it. Frank knows the original DNA results, and he can identify Rebecca. He never got a clear look at her face, but he at least heard her voice."

"Sounds like he isn't into cooperating, though."

"That was before. What does he care now? He's

already made his deal and told the truth. And then, somebody with law enforcement's level of access should be able to trace Rebecca's family back and fill in whatever blanks are left." I nodded firmly, as much to myself as to Snick. "Frank, family history, and family relationships that DNA can prove beyond question. That'll be more than enough to convict Rebecca."

I chewed at my thumbnail, and gave Snick a look that was probably very like the one a Victorian orphan boy has when he asks for more stew. "Don't you think? You think so, right?"

I never found out what he thought, because just as he opened his mouth to answer, a door slammed below us.

Footsteps came trotting up the stairs.

Funny. I knew we were safe up there, because I knew I would easily hear somebody on those old stairs. It never occurred to me to wonder what I'd do if the somebody didn't care whether I heard them or not.

There was only one way out of the attic, and that somebody was on it. We could either go down to meet them, or wait here.

Either way, we were trapped.

Chapter Twenty-One

Rebecca had a gun.

Snick made a squealing sound, a little like a frightened rodent, and backed up, hands raised like a bank robber.

I didn't move at all. I couldn't.

She had a gun.

I'd thought I was okay. Maybe not perfect, but okay. I'd certainly thought I was past the worst of it. But the sight of a gun, particularly one that was pointed at me, was a little much. My pulse was banging in my ears. My knees were weak. I was sweating.

I thought I might faint. I thought I might throw up.

Snick was the first to speak, his voice shrill. "You're *gone*!" It was kind of a silly thing to say, considering Rebecca was demonstrably not gone, but I supposed he was trying to get her talking. Stalling was never a bad idea, when somebody had a gun. "I *watched* you drive away!"

"You did." Rebecca's voice, on the other hand, was

entirely calm. "But you didn't watch me drive *back*, when I stopped for gas and realized I forgot my purse. I heard enough of your phone call to decide it was probably in my best interests to stay, preferably out of sight."

She waved her free hand. "I was going to miss my flight anyway. Security lines are *ridiculous* these days. Once Minerva got here, it wasn't hard to figure out where you went, with all the creaking and popping this place does."

Snick swore. "Stupid old house."

"So I gave you a good head start," said Rebecca, "and then I went up to my room."

"Stupid thin ceilings," he added.

Rebecca nodded. "Not just thin, but low on the old servants' level. A stepladder and a glass was all I needed." She shifted her cool gaze to me. "You got most everything right, if that makes you feel any better. A few details off here and there. I didn't steal his phone. We both set our phones down on a stump, to prove we weren't recording the conversation."

A smile drifted across her face. "He was pretty surprised, when he saw it was me. But it didn't seem to occur to him that I wouldn't have let him see it was me unless I intended to kill him."

"But you can't kill *us*!" Snick wailed. "How are you going to explain *that*?"

My only translatable thought was *gun gun gun gungungungun*. Which, while accurate, was not all that useful.

I did my best to get some marginal hold of myself. "He's—" I chirped. Then swallowed and started again, in something slightly more like a normal voice, even if it was trembling so hard I could barely understand myself. "He's right. It wouldn't look like an accident this time. And you'd never be able to hide our bodies before people started coming home."

"Why would I have to?" Rebecca asked. "Your bodies have nothing to do with *me*. I'm out of town."

This serenity of hers was not good. If she were panicked, impulsive, we might be able to talk her down and make her see how nitwitted this was. But if she was doing it deliberately, as a calculated choice, well. There wasn't much we could do to stop her.

What with her being the one with the gun.

But wasn't there something …?

Yes. There was something I needed to do. Or say. Something that would stop her.

Sadly, I had no idea what. My mind was moving like a jellyfish through ice.

I was definitely going to die.

I was going to die because she forgot her purse. Had she really just said she forgot her purse? I stared at the gun, and fought back an entirely inappropriate laugh. I should have known it was too good to be true, that she was leaving town. I should have known I could never be that lucky.

But honestly. Who forgets her purse? On her way to the *airport*?

At least I'd been smart enough not to bring Plant. *He* wasn't about to get shot. And if I disappeared, Gretchen would notice. She would go up and get him, and feed him. Plant would be fine.

I, on the other hand, would not be fine. Especially if I didn't get it together.

Think, Minerva. Think. Stop shaking and just think. Preferably about something other than Rebecca's purse.

"You can't get away with killing us," Snick said. "You know you can't. Probably we should just ..."

He kept talking, but I stopped listening—because I'd finally thawed out my brain enough to realize he was right.

She couldn't get away with killing us.

She just didn't know it yet.

"You don't have a sister!" I yelped.

Rebecca and Snick both looked at me—Snick even had to turn his head and take his eyes off Rebecca to do it—with almost identical expressions of befuddlement and irritation.

"What?" they both said at once.

"She doesn't have a sister," I said to Snick, because talking to him was easier than talking to the person with the gun. But since it was the person with the gun whom I most needed to hear me, I forced my gaze back to Rebecca. "You don't."

"Excellent ... sleuthing? I guess?" Rebecca was frowning and smiling at the same time. I guessed she thought I was having a nervous breakdown. Or else that I was just a complete nitwit. "Really cracked the case there, didn't you, hon?"

I lifted my chin. People treating me like a nitwit always got my dander up. Which was a good thing, in this case, because it helped quell my panic. A little. "I did, actually. That night I was talking to Snick about the burner phone, you were lurking in the hall. And you tried to cover it by saying your sister wouldn't stop texting you. But I called Carrie Kwon today, and she looked at your personnel file, from Tybryd. And she said you don't have a sister."

"What has this got to do with anything?" Rebecca asked, then laughed and went on before I could answer. "Yes, I took the burner phone from your room. We're a bit past that at this point, wouldn't you say?"

"Guess you should've taken Emily's journals, too," I said. "But that isn't the point either. The point is, I talked to Carrie. About you. This afternoon. Just before I came here." I arched my brows at her in what I hoped was a confident manner. Probably it was just a grimace of terror and death. But Snick was smiling now.

When Rebecca didn't immediately respond, I added, just in case she still didn't get it, "I told her things. Enough things that if Snick or I, or both of us, were suddenly to turn up missing, she would know enough to tell Ruby to look for *you*. And it wouldn't take Ruby long to find out you weren't on that flight."

"Sounds like it's over, Rebecca," said Snick. "The game's up, or whatever Sherlock Holmes says."

"The game's afoot," I corrected. "That's for the beginning of the mystery, not the end."

I guessed Rebecca didn't appreciate a pedant, because she raised the gun, steadied it with both hands, and pointed it at me.

"I thought we just established that there is no point in shooting me!" I squeaked. Just before my whole body seized up with panic.

"We did," Rebecca agreed. "But that doesn't mean it won't be fun."

"Rebecca—" Snick began, but she cut him off.

"If I'm going to jail either way, what's one more?"

With the kind of shrug you do when you're presented with two uninteresting options for dinner, and don't care which you eat, Rebecca fired.

Chapter Twenty-Two

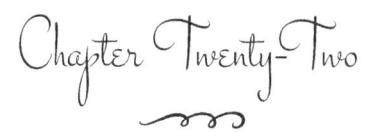

When I opened my eyes, with no memory of having closed them, Percy was there. Which, considering my probably atrocious breath and the definitely appalling state of my hair by that point, is not my favorite part of this story.

He was in a chair, by a bed—which I was in—but it wasn't my bed. He looked rumpled and a little pale and every bit as adorable as ever.

I looked blearily around. "Am I in the hospital?"

"Yep."

"Where's my dog?"

"He's fine. Gretchen has him. I was going to offer, but ..." He shrugged, his hand bouncing against his knee, which was also bouncing. He was tapping his foot, or something. Always in motion, that Percy Baird. "I wanted to be here when you woke up."

I narrowed my eyes at him. "Why?"

"Two reasons. Obviously because I rescued you, so you always want to know how that turns out—"

"You rescued me?"

His mouth dropped open. "You don't remember?"

"I remember ..." I tried to shrug, then winced as pain shot through my shoulder.

"Easy." He grabbed my hand, then seemed to notice he'd grabbed it, and dropped it again.

I frowned in place of the shrug. What did I remember? "Rebecca shot me, I guess. She shot me?"

"She did. Only in the shoulder, though, so it could've been worse. She wasn't much of a shot."

"It's harder than you think, having good aim." Something I'd learned. Natalie had almost killed me, but they told me that was more bad luck on my part than skill on hers. She didn't have a lot of experience with guns—the one she brought to my door that day was her husband's—and most people are naturally poor shots.

It sounded like my luck had been a lot better this time. As long as you didn't count Rebecca forgetting her stupid purse. "So the bullet didn't hit anything bad?"

Percy shook his head. "It'll hurt for a while, and you'll need help walking that giant goofball of yours, but other than that you'll be fine. I think shock and stress did you in as much as the bullet. It's getting late, but they said you can go home in the morning."

"How do you know all that?" I'd have liked to sit up straighter, so as to look properly accusatory, but my attempted shrug had taught me that moving too much was unwise. "Are they supposed to tell you that kind of thing, if you aren't my next of kin or whatever?"

A quick glance at the window—with eyes only—

showed it was full dark outside. "And why did they let you stay in here, if it's late?"

Percy waved a hand and vanished all questions with three words. "I'm a Baird."

I snorted. "I thought you were against taking advantage of wealth and power and all that."

His eyes softened. "Sometimes it's worth it."

I looked away, not liking what the expression on his face had just done to my stomach. I should have been mad about him rich-manning his way through my privacy (again), right?

I definitely should have been mad.

But I was not mad.

"And you rescued me?" I asked.

"Well, maybe *rescue* is a strong word, since you'd already been shot and all. But Elaine and I came home while you were up there, and we heard Snick shout." Percy scratched the back of his neck. "Took us a bit to find you guys. We thought the noise was coming from the staff level at first. But we got up there eventually, and I got the gun away from Rebecca."

As if presenting something, his hand sliced through the air. "And I carried you downstairs, while we waited for the ambulance."

I chose not to point out that you weren't actually supposed to move wounded people. Percy so loved a lady in distress, and I hated to burst his knightly bubble.

"I can't believe you don't remember." He crossed his arms and shook his head in mock disappointment. "I was a hero, and I get nothing for it?"

What did you want for it? was the first question that

popped into my head, but I refrained from asking it. Instead I asked, "What's the second reason you wanted to be here? You said there were two."

He leaned forward, elbows on his knees. Which meant I could smell him—soap, not cologne, which is exactly how a man should smell, in my opinion. But I wondered if that meant he could smell me too, and I shrank away. I was pretty sure I wasn't at my best.

"Because," he said, "I knew I was the only one around here who would realize exactly how bad it is for you, to be shot. I thought you'd be traumatized or something."

"I was. In the attic, I was. I'm sure I still will be, once it all sinks in. I feel a little out of it at the moment."

"That'd be the painkillers, I imagine. Anyway I thought you might need m—" Percy coughed and looked away. "I thought you might need a friend."

"Except we're not friends."

His eyes snapped back to mine, looking hurt.

"I gave them evidence against you!" I hastened to add. "I assumed you were mad at me."

"I was mad at you. Kind of." Percy held up his thumb and forefinger, an inch of space between them. "A little. But then you turned into this superhero who relentlessly pursued the truth and got shot to clear my name, so." He flashed the dimples. "Bygones."

I returned his smile. "What happened to Rebecca?"

"Not much, yet. I took her gun away—I don't know that she meant to do more shooting anyway, she seemed kind of deflated at that point—and I asked her if I needed to tie her up or something, or if she'd behave herself. She said she'd behave. And she did, for the most part, until Ruby took her away."

"I assume Snick told you everything?"

"I rode here in the ambulance with you, but he told Ruby everything, and she came by to tell me." Percy's knee started bouncing again, his fingers drumming against it. "You know, there'll have to be a whole trial and everything. I'm sure they'll need you to testify."

"I would think so."

"And anyway you should probably have consistent doctors or whatever, you know, while you're recovering. So you should probably stay. In Bryd Hollow."

My mind—and probably my face—went blank. Leaving hadn't occurred to me.

Maybe that was silly. The murders were solved now, and my whole screwup fixed. I guessed there wasn't anything keeping me here anymore, other than a low-paying job at a pet store that wasn't going to lead to much of a career.

Even so. "I have no intention of leaving."

"Good! That's good. I wish I could offer you your old job back, but ..." Percy gestured with one hand, as if waving my old job away.

"I didn't expect you to."

"My mother ... and living in the same ... I just think it'd be awkward. But there's a job at Tybryd opening up, if you want it."

"Event planning?" I asked with a laugh.

His brow furrowed. "How did you know?"

I gaped at him. "It really is event planning? I was

joking! Simone said that's where you put all the ex-PAs you don't know what to do with."

Was that what I was, here? Just another potential liability he was trying to neutralize?

"You talked to Simone?" he asked. "It's her job that's opening up. She's moving to Tennessee, says she's had enough of all of us. She didn't tell you?"

"We're not close or anything. I just talked to her about Frank." I tilted my head. "I'd be good at event planning, I think."

"You would. You did a good job with the ball, under some very difficult circumstances." Dimples again, just a little bit this time. "We'd have to get you some new dresses, maybe."

Highlight/lowlight of my first few weeks in Bryd Hollow: The lowlight was definitely getting shot. Again.

Getting fired from my brand new job wasn't so great either. Percy's arrest. Clifford kicking my dog. The whole murder thing. There were a lot of lowlights, actually.

There were plenty of highlights to go with them, though. Getting a new job at Tybryd was a good one. Plant not having to go to dog jail (for long), and not getting shot. Percy being there at the hospital was one too, but there has to be a point deduction for that thing with my breath and my hair.

And then there was him turning back to me, hand on the door handle, just before he left the room:

"So. Plans for the weekend?"

I blinked at him. "Recovering from a gunshot wound."

"Right." He tugged at his ear. "Well, I had this thing

on Monday, but I'm pretty sure that's canceled. All the sudden my weekend's wide open. I could help you with Plant."

"Oh!" I tried not to look too excited. Was there dirty laundry on my floor? And if so, would I be able to clean it up, with one functioning arm? "That would be really nice of you. Plant would love to see you."

"Great." He crossed back to the bed and dropped a lightning-quick kiss on the top of my head. "I'll bring you some fries."

Dear Reader

Thank you for reading *Mystery Repeats Itself*. I hope you enjoyed it! Minerva's next adventure is *Old Knives Tale*.

If you'd like to know when I've got a new book, be sure to sign up for my newsletter at cordeliarook.com. You'll find my email address there as well; I love to hear from readers!

Your honest ratings and reviews help other readers choose books. I hope you'll consider giving your opinion at your online retailer.

Minervaisms

butter upon bacon: even more of a good thing; over the top; an extravagance

carriwitchet: a befuddling question; a puzzle

fizzing: excellent; impressive

hornswaggler: a fraud or cheat

nanty-narking: having great fun; partying

odsbodikins: an all-purpose expression of dismay, surprise, or irritation, similar to "Oh my gosh!" or "Gosh darnit!"

pantry politicking: gossiping among the household, staff, or servants

podsnappery: a refusal to recognize the unpleasant; complacency

ratbag: a jerk; a sleazy person

Made in the USA
Monee, IL
07 December 2022